I0776674

THE CURSES COLLECTION

WRITTEN BY
JOHN WAYNE COMUNALE

ILLUSTRATED BY
MIKE DUBISCH

THE
CURSES
COLLECTION

WRITTEN BY
JOHN WAYNE COMUNALE

ILLUSTRATED BY
MIKE DUBISCH

CURSES

JOHN WAYNE IS ALIVE
BY SAM RICHARD

If you've been to many horror conventions over the past few years, there's a good chance you've met John Wayne. And if you've met him, there's also a good chance that you bought a book, smoked some weed, and/or shot the shit with him. It's almost impossible not to. The dude is fucking personable.

He's also a fantastic and prolific writer, pushing out 10+ books in the past handful of years. And the shit's good, weird, often funny, and usually horrific. A lot of it is gross too, but all of it has heart. He rides this perfect line between horror and bizarro that's twisted and unique.

And I never know what he's gonna do next. Each book is as strange and different as the last, like he's allergic to recycling ideas. But what I hadn't ever seen from John Wayne was a collection of short fiction. And I knew the guy had scattered pieces in anthologies and magazines throughout the years. I always wondered if he was ever gonna pull the trigger on that. Well, now you're holding it. And unsurprisingly, it's very fucking good. And weird. And often funny. And usually horrific. And a lot of it is gross. But all of it has heart.

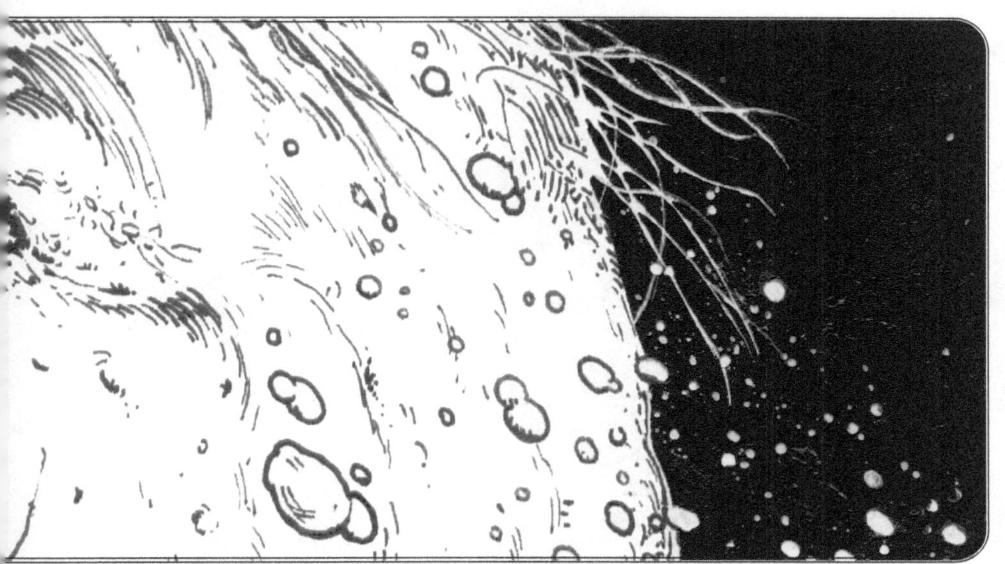

Basically everything I hoped and expected it would be. I've known John Wayne for something like 8 years at this point. We became friends over beers and conversation at BizarroCon 2015 (or maybe 2016…?). He's one of my favorite people to hang out with at the bar after days of tabling are done. When I've hit that point of not wanting to talk to anyone else because I've been selling books to strangers for 10 hours and my brain is jelly. But that doesn't seem to happen to John Wayne. Dude is like a fucking machine. Boundless energy. Shit is uncanny.Over the years, I've watched his career grow and expand. And the thing is, he was killing it from the beginning.

I still think about *Aunt Poster*, one of his very first books. Shit stuck with me for its unflinching exploration of the awkwardness of budding sexuality unlike anything I've ever read.But now we're here, in 2023, and he's still cranking out killer book after killer book. And this one? Well it's no fucking different. However, being a collection, you now get to see him with all his range on display in one place. It's an impressive feat. All the stories feel like John Wayne, but they're all so different. And all of them have heart.

Thanks for picking this book up. I hope you like it as much as I did. I also hope reading it encourages you to check out more of his books if you haven't. Because the dude is fucking good. ☠

THE BLACK DRAPE

People have told me I was meaner than the devil himself, and I wouldn't disagree. The only difference is the devil's not real, and I am. People called Jerry Lee Lewis *The Killer*, but it was a nickname, and around the house, he was just plain ol' Jerry Lee. I got called mean so many times it became my name, Mean. Hell, I forgot my given name long ago, not that it mattered. Mean suits me just fine.

I prefer to think I'm more direct than mean, but I guess that depends on one's perception. I've been at this a long time and have no problem being mean, especially when it's called for, which is pretty much always.

The only thing I ever wanted to do was play, and my desire was fulfilled years ago in San Francisco at a venue known for mysterious occurrences. A place known as The Black Drape.

A lot of things happen at that place, and not one of them is good, but most people learn to make peace with their decisions. Those who can't don't last very long. It could be looked at as culling the herd or eliminating the weak, but sometimes, I think they were the smart ones. Making death deals at The Black Drape isn't uncommon, but simply seeking the place out was tantamount to death. They don't realize how much harder they have to work once they get what they want, and they thought they were working hard before.

That's what breaks them, the work, but there's always a price to pay for what you're given, especially when The Black Drape gives it to you. Take me, for instance; all I wanted to do was play for people. I loved it so much that my fingers would itch if they spent too much time away from the piano keys. The instrument was a detachable extension of my hand, and we could only be separated for a short time before my fingers ached to reconnect.

I got tired of acquiescing to piano players who didn't have half my talent just because they'd been around longer. I didn't want to wait fifteen or twenty years before earning the seniority required to gig regularly. I wanted to play now, and I wanted to play every night. The deal I made in the shadows of The Black Drape on that night so many years ago allowed me to do just that, but not without a 'by the way'.

Your life is the only thing worth a shit to the scourge who conducts business at the club and, therefore, a part of every deal. The conditions are unique to the individual, but what is taken in trade is always the same. With my deal, I didn't *get* to play every night. I *had* to play every night. If I didn't, I was dead. It was that simple.

There were rules, just as there always are, with deals like these made in the club's dark corners. For me, it wouldn't be as easy as becoming a house musician playing nightly at whatever club happened to be deemed 'swanky' at the time. The conditions of my deal forbade me to ever play in the same place twice. I would have to keep traveling to different bars, venues, and speakeasies from night to night perpetually, on the road for eternity.

The consolation for my trouble was as long as I made it before show time, I would be included on the bill as if I were expected to be there all along. I understood if a night went by where I didn't play a gig, I was toast, only it took a while for the totality to sink in. I couldn't die unless I stopped playing.

The Black Drape had given me what I wanted with a damned if I do, damned if I don't clause attached. They get their payment one way or another, only I'm the one who decides when I'm ready to pay in full. I know it sounds cliché to say I've been doing this longer than I can remember, but there's no other way for me to say it.

I stopped paying attention to the passage of time after making the deal. I wasn't affected by it the same way anymore, and it was an unbelievable relief to cast off the weight of that unstoppable beast. I didn't enjoy it for long as it was replaced by the heavier burden of choosing when to die so long as I found a gig every night, which was easy at first.

It didn't take long for there to start being more and more distance between the places I could play. They were testing me. They were hungry for payment, but I couldn't let them decide. I would choose when to die, not some 'shadow men' who thought they got the best of me. I forged on unfazed by miles, weather, or bad luck. Then, strange things started to happen when I played.

I didn't pick up on it right away since I was focused on playing and making it to the next gig on time, but when I realized I had something to do with the strange occurrences happening around me, others did, too. Nothing could be pinned on me, but you'd have to be blind not to see I had a hand in the chaos.

One night, I was playing and noticed the patrons get up and take their drinks back to the bar. A commotion started when the bartender/owner got into a shouting match with one of them. I was aware but didn't let it distract me, and I remained focused on my playing. When I was settling up afterward, I asked about what happened earlier in the evening and what all the shouting was about.

He told me the beer was spoiled, not just some of it. Every barrel of beer the barkeep tapped yielded an undrinkable, thick, sour concoction unsuitable for consumption. I didn't ask, but the man told me he intended to give the brewers a piece of his mind. He'd demand they replace all the barrels and reimburse him for his lost business. I muttered a half-audible *good luck* before slipping out into the night.

The next evening, while I played, a drunk man in the audience talked loudly to the women across from him through most of the set and eventually passed out at the table. When I'd played my last song, the folks around him discovered he hadn't put his head down because he was drunk. He was dead.

A few nights later, a waitress brought the glass of whiskey I ordered to the stage. I took a drink; it was gin instead, my least favorite spirit. I fumed internally for the rest of the set without finishing the vile liquor. When I got off stage, the bar was crowded with cocktails that had been sent back. It turned out all the whiskey tasted like gin, but every liquor in the bar tasted like toilet water. The owner was beside himself when I collected my payment and slunk out through the back.

The rumors started shortly after, or maybe they'd already begun.

Other piano men warned me about The Black Drape, ones who quit when age, arthritis, and an innumerable amount of unjust yet inevitable ailments robbed them of their gift. Be careful what I wish for, they told me. They said sometimes what you love the most, your life's true passion, can become a grinding job in the blink of an eye.

I ignored their advice and wrote them off as bitter old fools whose careers took them no farther than their local watering hole. They were jealous of my discipline, drive, and ambition to be more than they could imagine. I didn't see what could be so bad about playing music as a job. It was my dream to play for a living. I'd much rather tickle the ivory nightly than take on any number of physical labor jobs, the only kind I was otherwise qualified for.

I refused to believe them until one night when I sat down to play in the pub of a small mountain town I'd happened upon. I took a breath and launched into the intro of my first number, plunking lightly on the high notes, keeping them soft and airy until the main theme kicked in like thunder when I really started banging on the keys. That was all I remembered about the set until I found myself striking the last chord of the final song.

I had completely tuned out the entire time I played without realizing it. I couldn't remember what I was thinking about, so it couldn't have been important. The worst part was I felt nothing. Until then, whenever I played one song or ten, I was always left with a unique feeling of warmth deep inside. A sense I equated with the accomplishment of being one with what I was doing. After that show, the feeling was gone, and in its place was an empty ache.

It was another test, and I knew it. Those shady deal makers thought they could hasten me to the end by sucking away the joy I felt from performing my craft. They were laying it on, with gigs becoming harder to find, and now toying with my emotions. Instead of demoralizing me as these things were intended to do, I was motivated. They could do their best to break my spirit, but it would take more to bring me down, a lot more.

The strange happenings associated with my music became a given, and word of my reputation spread. One night, I showed up at a pub in a small village at the base of a mountain pass to play, but there was no piano waiting for me.

"I was under the impression you were bringing your own piano," said the mustachioed barkeep.

"And *what*," I sneered through clenched teeth, "gave you that impression?"

It was a question I knew he didn't have an answer for, and the barkeep just stared blankly back at me as if waiting for me to respond to myself. Part of the deal was making it to a venue every night where a gig would always await me. Now, the gig was here, but no way for me to play it. Those slimy bastards were anxious for payment, but I still would not relent.

"How long until I go on," I finally said.

"Oh, about twenty minutes or so, I suppose," the man answered as if we hadn't just talked about no piano. "Can I get you something while you wait?"

His smile was obnoxious and tobacco-yellowed teeth poked out from beneath the bushy, brown moustache. If his brain weren't being scrambled by dark forces, I would've knocked every crooked yellow tooth out of that shit-eatin' grin. It wasn't his fault, though, and I knew it but decided if I didn't find a piano in time, I would do it anyway as a parting gift to myself before being dragged off into the void.

"I'll be back," I spat as I pushed through the lazy saloon-style doors into the street.

It was cold, and it wasn't snowing as earlier. Scattered, wet, white patches covered small portions of the street and collected in ivory mounds on the slanted roofs across from the bar. The wind blew down the road in frigid gusts, piercing the layers I wore like thousands of icy needles.

I pulled my collar tight around my neck and angled my hat's brim down to keep the howling, frozen wind out of my eyes. I stepped out into the street and scanned the surrounding buildings until I found the town's general store. I braced against the wind, crossed the street, and went in, heading immediately to the back wall.

It didn't take long to find a long chain thick enough for what I had in mind, and I was back at the counter before the shopkeeper could ask if I needed help. I grunted as I walked past him, winding the chain, looping it around my shoulder, and threw a handful of bills in his direction on my way to the door.

"Keep the change," I growled, stepping back into the street.

I turned left and headed straight for the steeple I spotted peeking out over the rooftops at the end of the street when I arrived. Acquiring the chain didn't take much time, but I put a little more hitch in giddy-up.

I lowered my shoulder into the church door, and it fell easier than a drunk after the last call. A portly preacher came rushing through the billowing dust, hollering, but I dipped my other shoulder into his chest as I passed him coming down the aisle. He lay on the ground, clutching his spasming stomach and struggling to gulp air.

As I'd expected, an old upright piano was to the left of the pulpit, and I ripped it away from the wall. The rusty casters it rolled on whined in protest of being moved, but I ignored their shrill, jarring squeal. I wrapped the chain around the piano twice and still had a dozen feet left after tying off the end.

I spit on my hands and picked up the end of the chain as another man of the cloth frantically entered the sanctuary. He tried to help his fellow preacher up from the floor with one hand and cast me out like I was the devil with the other. The first preacher still couldn't catch his breath and flailed in the arms of his would-be savior.

I gave the chain a solid yank, and the piano slid across the pulpit to me. The rusted-out wheels gashed deep grooves into the polished wood floor, and I couldn't help but grin. The thing probably hadn't been moved since it was put in that spot fifty or so years ago, and the lack of upkeep showed. I folded the keys cover and found some were broken into jagged pieces and others stuck in the down position. None of that mattered as long as the piano and I got back down the street to the bar before time ran out.

The second priest gave up helping his colleague and approached me with one hand extended as the other clutched a pocket-sized Bible. He kept blabbering on and begging Jesus to make me go away, and I was desperate to oblige. I brought the fingers on my right hand down hard on the keys, striking a half-sour, warbling E major chord.

The sustain was for shit on the old thing, but the desired result was enough to halt the advancing preacher. His eyes went too wide for his skull, and he made a break for the door, pulling his partner along with him. I proceeded down the aisle, dragging the piano behind me amidst portraits of Jesus and Mary crying tears of blood as I passed.

I got to the door and pulled until the piano snapped the frame and tore through the front of the building. Another hefty tug brought it rolling down the few stairs and into the street with me. The clock hanging over the bank's door across the street told me my remaining time was in the low single digits.

I gritted my teeth and fixed the angle of my hat again to keep the flurries out of my eyes. The second preacher was running up the street, hollering something awful, leaving his friend leaning up against the deck across the front of the church. He turned back to look, stumbled on a patch of snow, and landed face-first in a pile of half-frozen slush. I paid no mind as I pulled the piano down the road, my hands blistered and bloody from the chain.

The preacher rolled over on his back, grabbed his chest, and moaned like a wounded animal. I kept my head down as I approached with the piano in tow, and he'd just managed to catch his breath and get to his knees. I glanced over and saw him looking past me, eyes wide and bleary with terror, mouth hanging open like a soundless 'no'.

I saw flames reflected in the tears pooling at the base of his eyes and turned to look over my shoulder. The church was burning, and the preacher leaning up against the deck was burning along with it. Residual vibrations from the chord I'd struck couldn't find a way out through the ceiling, so they made one.

I turned my head forward and kept pulling. It wasn't the first church I'd made burn, and it wouldn't be the last.

A few concerned town folks dashed past me toward the burning church and paid no attention to the man dragging a piano by a chain. When I reached the pub and climbed the stairs to the door, I still had one minute to spare.

"There you are," said the barkeep. "There's some kind of trouble up the street at the church. I was afraid you'd gotten held up by the all the hubbub."

I said nothing and focused solely on getting the piano to the stage so I could start playing on time.

"A-are you okay?" The barkeep's face twisted with confusion. "You sure are awful sweaty, and your face is—"

He was cut off by the crashing clatter as I dragged the piano up the wooden steps from the street and into the bar. He ducked his head and covered his ears against the destructive commotion until I had the piano through the doors. It knocked them from the hinges and splintered the frame like the church, but it didn't necessarily make the shithole any worse.

On the way to the stage, I pulled the piano through the few tables and chairs sparse with patrons, some of which were displaced as the chained instrument carved an indiscriminate path through the limited seating area. The barkeep made a hell of a stink and started yelling, but I couldn't hear over the clattering tables and chairs.

The metal wheels beneath the standup piano had become sharp and pointy from being dragged along the road, and they had cut four deep grooves into the wood plank floor of the bar from the door to the stage. Small, curly wood shavings ejected from the long divots that swirled and danced across the floor on an icy breeze blowing through the widened door. Something about it reminded me of when I stood outside The Black Drape, trying to work up the courage to make my deal.

The few patrons present were confused by what I was doing, and the barkeep kept opening his mouth to say something but stopped short each time like a cork stuck in his throat that kept his protests from getting by.

The stage was just a touch shy of four feet high, and the narrow planks turned makeshift stairs wouldn't hold the instrument's weight. I dropped the chain and wiped blood from broken blisters on my pants. I wrapped my arms around the piano from the back and gripped the sides firmly.

By my estimation, I had a few seconds to start playing, or I'd be paying up with my life. I bent my knees, held on tight, lifted the piano over my head, and tossed it on the stage. The padded hammers inside bounced against their corresponding strings, sounding random, dissonant notes against the crash of the breaking wood. Planks cracked, buckled, and broke under the impact, and the chain landed in a jumbled pile next to the piano with a jangly hiss.

I leapt to the stage and took one long stride over the busted planks, my arms extended, my fingers outstretched and poised to play. I glanced over my shoulder to see the speechless bartender hastily push past stunned customers on his way to the stage. My feet hit the floor in front of the piano, and as I drew in my breath to count off the opening number, a man ran in from the street, hollering.

"Everyone, come help!" He attempted to sound authoritative, but his voice lacked the proper timbre. "The church is burning down, and the preacher's burning up with it!"

The patrons broke for the door to follow the man outside, with the barkeep bringing up the rear. He was a step away from the door when he glanced back, and I struck the first chord of the song.

I stood at that old church piano and played my entire set to an empty bar. The songs carried out into the street and played background music to the chaos I created. I finished, and there was no applause or encores, only panicked screaming from outside. The fire spread and was working its way down the street toward the bar.

I reached down for the chain, stepped off the front of the stage, and headed out, dragging the piano behind me. It fit through the door much easier this time but still pulled the rest of the frame away as it came through.

The street was filled with townsfolk running around screaming while trying unsuccessfully to prevent the fire's progress. Their attempted bucket brigade was disorganized, with wide gaps in which water was spilled and wasted. I imagined there wouldn't be much left of the town by morning, but I wouldn't be back regardless.

I hooked a left, dragging the piano behind the bar where I could access the mountain pass. It was the only other way out of town that didn't involve walking through the inferno that had spread to both sides of the street. I could still hear the townsfolk wailing from a good two hundred yards away, and I saw the flames until the mountain itself eclipsed my view.

I decided to drag the piano with me to the next gig. I had a feeling I'd need it. The shadow men of The Black Drape couldn't collect their payment, but they were clamoring for it now, and the piano thing was just the start. It would surely get much more difficult from here, but that didn't mean I would make it easy for them.

Soon, the blisters would go thick and rough with calluses to protect my hands against the chain, and lugging the piano everywhere would only make me stronger.

I don't know what else The Black Drape would throw at me in the next small village tucked away in the valley ahead, but I'm bringing fire in my belly, a chip on my shoulder, and my goddamn piano. Hell, this might even make this job fun again for me. ☠

COLLECTION DAY

he ragged bodega was dilapidated to the extent you'd think it was condemned if it weren't for a sign on the door proclaiming it was 'Open'. This was Johnny's last stop for the day, and it was no accident either. He looked up at the single-room apartment above the old store and inadvertently shuddered. The windows were covered by thick black tapestries to block out any light that might find its way through the outer layer of filth.

It was cold and rainy, but the temperature had nothing to do with the chill he felt standing there. Johnny made Adria's place his last stop because she gave him the creeps in a big, bad way. He didn't scare easily, which was why he was so good at his job, but something about the old Cuban woman didn't sit right with him. He wouldn't say he was afraid of her because fear didn't accurately describe the feeling.

After each interaction, a dark, disquieting vibe radiated from the woman, leaving Johnny with a bad taste in his mouth. On bad days, he could taste her for hours afterward.

Johnny didn't like Adria, but she was a good customer for his boss, Sal. Sal wasn't interested in what Johnny thought and couldn't care less about his comfort in dealing with the woman. It was all about money for Sal, and being that Johnny was a low-level associate in one tiny aspect of a much larger 'business', he knew better than to share his feelings about anything.

Sal and his business partners had run the numbers game in Johnny's neighborhood since he was a kid. His own mother was a devoted daily player to the extent that he didn't realize it was something out of the ordinary. He was under the impression everyone made a daily phone call with their pick, hoping to win big. Sal and his associates were regular guests of Johnny and his mother, and, with his father out of the picture, the kid looked up to them as the sole male role models in his life.

Johnny didn't know exactly what Sal did when he was younger, but for as long as he could remember, he'd hoped to work for the man one day. He told his mother so on several occasions on which she would always nod and say, "We'll see Johnny. We'll see."

And see, she did. She saw Sal give Johnny small jobs when he became a teenager, mostly running simple errands like getting him and 'the boys' coffee and meals and picking up their dry cleaning. It was just small-time stuff in the beginning. After a few years, Johnny saw more than enough to know what kind of business Sal was in and wanted to be in it, too. Hence, he was given his first real job as a collector. This entailed Johnny visiting roughly the same people daily to collect the money they lost playing the number that day, and on the rare occasion that someone on his route won, he'd drop off their winnings.

Everyday, people in the neighborhood bet on a three-digit number determined by the amount of money the horse track made on that particular day, and if the number you chose matched the last three digits of that sum, you won. It was that simple.

Johnny stood outside Adria's bodega getting soaked, and with his leather blazer doing little to protect him, he begrudgingly entered the store. Inside was dark, with only a few lights on toward the back where the lone register sat atop a counter covered in dust and rat droppings. The two aisles of the store were empty save for a few random badly dented canned goods, some packs of ramen, and several bags of expired generic potato chips.

On a shelf behind the register were large glass jars containing various herbs, dried leaves, and unrecognizable things of which Johnny did not want to know the origin. Behind the counter sat a young, dark-skinned Cuban girl named Celia. She was thumbing through a magazine on the counter before her and couldn't be bothered to look up.

"She's upstairs," the girl said. "She's expecting you."

The words reignited his anxiety, particularly the inflection she said "expecting." Johnny attempted to stifle a shiver with no luck and spasmodically shook as he approached the counter.

"It's chilly out there today," he said, trying to play it off, but Celia didn't notice or care.

Johnny tried to flirt with Celia the first few times he visited Adria's. Flirting was like a reflex he couldn't help, and while she was cute and all, he was just playing the odds. The more women he talked to, the better his chance of them being interested in him.

Celia was ice cold and blew him off before he could speak. He didn't mind a challenge and was determined, at the very least, to get her to smile. Johnny stopped trying after he discovered what happened in the room upstairs.

The entrance to the stairs was in the small office behind the counter, and Johnny stepped through the beaded curtain that acted as a door. Adria didn't have items to sell in her bodega because she didn't need any. She was, for lack of a better term, the neighborhood witch doctor, and people sought her out for all kinds of help they believed she could provide through her sacred Santeria rituals.

Being a witch doctor wasn't illegal and did not require a front like a bodega. Still, Adria wasn't practicing the spiritual rituals you advertise with a flashing neon palm in the window. She engaged in ancient practices some would find dangerous and irresponsible, but the buffer of a fake business kept the unsuspecting at arm's length.

The office was small and dark, and the stale stench of sage hung thick in the air on the verge of resolidifying. Johnny fully expected to walk into the office one day and bang his head on a hard resin cloud of stink. His eyes watered, and his nose played the copycat, each trying to push out more liquid than the other in a misery-driven competition.

He looked around for a tissue, napkin, or even a paper towel but could only find a wadded t-shirt pushed into the back corner of a filth-covered desk. The shirt had been there since Johnny started, and the fabric had gone stiffer than a teenage boy's secret gym sock. Johnny wiped his nose and eyes on his sleeve as he ducked through a second beaded curtain hiding the stairs.

The single, standard, thirteen-step staircase up to Adria's room stopped at a small landing where a man named Jesus would sit on a stool to make sure no one decided to drop by uninvited. Jesus carried two silver nine millimeters tucked quite conspicuously into his pants to deter anyone from trying to get 'cute' with him.

Today, Johnny stood at the bottom of the stairs, looking up to the landing at Jesus's empty stool. Jesus was always there, always. While they gave Johnny another reason to feel uneasy, he was able to rationalize away his fear. He had to take a break sometime and was probably just in the can. Besides, if something were wrong, Celia would have let him know. At least, he hoped she would, but he wasn't sure the girl had his best interests at heart.

He contemplated walking back out through the store and leaving for a moment. Maybe he could come back later or even push the pickup off until tomorrow, depending on whether Sal was in a good mood. Johnny looked from the beaded curtain to the stairs and back again before shaking off the feeling of dread. He was being stupid, or at least he convinced himself he was.

He had no reason to be scared of collecting gambling debts from an old woman regardless of the dark powers over which she may or may not hold dominion. It had nothing to do with the business she did with Sal. Johnny reached into his jacket and fingered the pistol handle holstered around his side to reinvigorate his confidence.

"Last stop," Johnny whispered to himself. "Last stop."

He climbed the wooden steps but didn't remember them creaking as much or as loudly before today. He wrote it off as something he never noticed because he usually talked with Jesus on his way up. Everything sounds louder and different than you remember against a backdrop of silence.

Halfway up, Johnny swore he heard the beaded curtain at the bottom of the stairs rattle with a sway invoked by entry. He whirled around with one hand going for his gun and the other reaching for the banister as the quick turn threw him off balance.

No one was there, and while relieved, Johnny was aggravated with himself. He needed to get his shit together and get it the fuck together *now*. To collect his money and leave. He took the remaining stairs two at a time and knocked on the door as soon as his foot hit the landing.

"Adria, it's Johnny," he called as he knocked. "I'm in a hurry today, so just . . . just, I'm in a hurry is all so—"

Johnny trailed off, expecting to be interrupted any second by the door opening or Adria shouting back at him from the other side. Still, nothing happened. Johnny knocked again harder this time, his aggravation turning to agitation.

"Adria," he called again. "I know you're up here. Celia told me you knew I was coming."

He pounded the door harder and faster, matching the pounding in his chest.

"Open up Adria! Open u—"

The door swung open, revealing a dark, distorted scene of shapes and shadows. Wafts of incense smoke hovered around the flames of the few candles that provided light in the small, shadowy space. The odor was unlike any spice or weed he'd smelled the old woman burn on prior visits. Whatever this was smelled salty with a sharp bitterness that burned Johnny's nostrils like wasabi.

His eyes watered, and his nostrils sting hurt his head. He stuck his hand out to lean on the doorframe and pinched the bridge of his nose, squinting against tears.

"Jesus, Adria," Johnny coughed. "What the hell?"

He stepped through the door, rubbing his eyes and waving clouds of the stink away from his face. Johnny ventured another step but stopped when he ran into something at his feet. When he stepped back, his shoe came out from the sticky floor with a slow, slurpy wetness, and in the tiny rectangle of light spilling through the open door, Johnny saw what tripped him up. It was a goat's head that had recently been separated from a body he couldn't see but could smell.

Then, things began to happen very fast.

Johnny looked up through the smoky, dim light, trying to make out as much of the room as the limited visibility would allow. Shock turned his feet to bricks, and his tongue became an immovable lead-filled weight. His brain sent signals to his hands urging them to grab the holstered gun, but Johnny's extremities weren't accepting any calls.

He assumed the blood he'd stepped in had come from the goat's head, but there was too much of it to have come from only one goat. Johnny wanted to make sense of what he was seeing. He wanted there to be an explanation. He needed there to be one.

Johnny didn't know much about Santeria, but he'd heard they killed animals during certain rituals, so the goat head made sense. What didn't make sense was the severed head of Jesus sitting atop the circular table at the center of the room, his mouth agape, wearing a forever-frozen expression of surprise.

Adria was on her knees at the table facing Johnny, but she no longer resembled the old woman from whom he collected each week. Her head was down with her chin against her chest, but only the front half of her head. The back half fell in the opposite direction, split open from the top to her shoulders.

One of the candles near the table gave Johnny a clear view of the inside of Adria's head. Light danced around wet red pulp, and her brain was missing or pulverized into grey mush.

Johnny didn't realize he could move again until he'd already taken a step toward the table. Everything within him screamed in protest against this move, but he couldn't help it. As terrifying as the scene was, Johnny couldn't fight the compulsion to take a closer look.

A thin waterfall of blood leaked soundlessly off the side of the table from the back of Jesus's head. The puddle was deep closer to the table, and Johnny's footstep caused a ripple that crested over the toe of his shoe. He cringed as blood seeped through his sock, slicking the spaces between his toes. There was something in Jesus's mouth that Johnny couldn't see until he stepped closer. It was round, but the light was too low to make out any other detail.

From the corner of his eye, Johnny caught a glimpse of a hand, flinched, and threw his arms up in anticipation of being hit. When the blow didn't come, he lowered his guard slowly and squinted into the darkness. He was right about seeing a hand but was in no danger.

It was severed at the wrist and hung from a hook at the end of a chain attached to the ceiling. The roof of the building was pitched, and the other end of the chain disappeared into the darkness of the steep angle. He looked down and saw other body parts hanging from hooks across the room.

Just beyond the hand was an arm cut at the shoulder. The lacerated flesh hung in uneven, jagged strips, signifying that the cuts were not done with patience or precision. Johnny got a good enough look to notice several tattoos positively identifying the rest of Jesus dangling from the ceiling around him. Now, all the blood made sense.

He was overwhelmed, but taking in the details rocked his equilibrium. He grabbed the empty chair that was pushed out and back from the table like someone had been there but left before death exploded across the room. Or maybe they left after?

Johnny leaned hard on the chair to keep his balance while successfully navigating the tidal wave of nausea crashing down on him. His wits were returning. Whatever compelled him to investigate the room had been beaten back by common sense far enough for him to know he didn't want to be there anymore.

He held fast to the chair, fighting the sudden amplification of gravity demanding his obedience. The chair looked old, like an antique, and he thought it sat too high for a table so low, but maybe it was supposed to be that way.

Johnny noticed something else about the chair as his fingers clawed deeply into the soft leather upholstery. It was dry. Everything in the small room, from floor to ceiling, had been touched by blood except this chair. Before he could invent scenarios in which this made sense, something caught his eye just beyond the gently swinging torso of Jesus.

There was a statue of a saint, but it wasn't the three-foot, crudely painted, fiberglass visage of Saint Lazarus Johnny saw every other time he'd visited Adria. This one stood twice as tall, and the usually brightly colored robes were replaced by thick and heavy, tattered, black rags.

The eyes were rimmed red, and the mouth was a frozen snarl, baring horrifically realistic fangs. Dancing flames on candles around the statue's feet blinked in and out as if communicating through code.

Johnny didn't realize he'd started vomiting until he looked down and saw the chair that he was holding. It may have somehow avoided being soaked in blood like the rest of the room, but it was not spared from the partially digested sludge that had been Johnny's lunch of ham and eggs hours earlier.

"Goddamnit."

Surprised, Johnny snapped his head up and spit stray chunks across the table at the partially bifurcated Cuban woman.

"Do you have any idea how hard it was to keep from getting blood on that chair?" The voice was coming from behind him. "All that trouble just to have you ruin it with your Ginny puke!"

Johnny turned in the direction of the voice coming from over his shoulder, scared shitless of who or what was talking to him. His hands shook too badly to grab his gun, so he would have to face the situation unarmed and hope his strength returned.

"I thought guys like you had seen it all and wouldn't be bothered by . . . a little blood."

Johnny squinted through the lowlight and saw Celia, the young Cuban girl who watched the store. He went to reply, but his stomach lurched and swallowed hard against rising bile.

"In case you haven't already realized it, Johnny," Celia continued. "You're not going to be collecting your money today."

She opened her mouth well beyond the point her jaw should have allowed, her monstrous maw reminding him of sharks he'd seen on nature programs. Rows of pointy crooked knives masquerading as teeth filled her mouth, but lurking just beyond them was nonsensical chaos.

Black and red smoke swirled at the opening of her throat, backlit by flames from somewhere deep inside. It spun over Celia's bottom lip and danced slowly to the floor, bouncing toward Johnny.

Smoke continued pushing its way out of Celia's throat and quickly closed the distance between them. Johnny saw faces within the cloud, morphing in and out of momentary existence, mouths open in silent screams.

He wanted to move. He tried to run and knew he should, but the smoke danced so that he couldn't stop looking. The free-flowing motion mesmerized him and kept him from acting on the impulse.

The twirling plume paused within inches of his face. Thin, gnarled fingers shot from the translucent black cloud-piercing his body where they wrapped around adrenaline-soaked insides and pulled down. The air squeezed from his lungs, and his knees buckled from the sudden intense pressure against his organs.

Johnny gasped for air he could no longer draw and could hear Celia's laughter from deep within the hellishly misshapen vortex. He felt something twist and then pop inside him, and his knees gave up, trying to keep him on his feet. He couldn't see, hear, or feel anything as he fell to the blood and vomit-soaked floor.

Unfortunately, his senses returned too quickly, bringing blurry shapes of horror back into focus. A high-pitched ring screamed through his head, growing louder and higher until warm wetness found its way out of his ears and ran down the sides of his face. The pressure inside his body refused to subside, and Johnny could only hug his chest while fighting to gulp down the air.

Celia stood over him now.

Maybe it was the flickering candlelight accenting her soft and delicate features or the angle from which he was looking. However, even in this terrifying situation, Johnny still found something intangibly attractive about the girl.

He tried to call out and demand to know what the hell was going on, but he could only cough up the alkaline-flavored slickness with which his lungs were quickly filling up. He watched helplessly as her Cheshire smile grew wide. She was re-opening the cavernous portal responsible for what was currently crushing his insides like the creeping hydraulics of a trash compactor.

This was not the coy Cuban girl Johnny assumed was playing hard to get. This was something else.

He rolled back and away, splashing through the warm goulash of co-mingled bodily fluids until he smacked against the table, knocking over a nearby candle.

The impact pushed the edge into the belly of the witch's carcass, causing it to sway. As the momentum settled, the front half of Adria's face slowly curled down and over itself like a lid being pulled from a can of sardines with the wet whisper of two slices of spoiled ham being torn apart.

Johnny stared up into the fang-filled smile carved sloppily into Celia's face. He'd stumbled upon a nightmare come to life from which he badly wished to wake. His train of thought diverted suddenly when something round and wet fell on his chest.

Jesus's head looked up from Johnny's lap through dead eyes, his twisted final expression resting somewhere between and confused.

Johnny couldn't move. He didn't even realize he'd stopped breathing.

Black spots dotted his vision and quickly ballooned into a bank of eclipsing clouds swirling around like ink dropped into a bucket of water. If the thing in Jesus's mouth hatched, Johnny didn't see what it was. He couldn't see the grotesquely deformed thing he knew as Celia standing over him anymore, nor could he hear cackling from a mouth jammed with razor teeth.

Johnny's organs finally ruptured, mercifully granting him a death he happily welcomed. In the final flickers of life, his thoughts turned not to his family, loved ones, or even a montage of life events but instead to Sal. He was going to be pissed Johnny didn't get his money.

Celia leaned against the bodega counter, flipping through a fashion magazine from three months prior. The only current publications they carried in the 'store' were books used to interpret dreams into numeric form for gambling purposes. If she wanted a recent magazine, she had to walk to the newsstand at the corner, but she hadn't left the bodega in months.

She'd ventured out only a few times since Adria freed her from the realm she'd been bound for countless years but preferred to stay in the bodega and let those she dealt with come to her. This was how she'd done business before her imprisonment, and this was how she intended to continue now on her own terms.

The ancient, warbling cry of an old landline telephone ruined the silence of the otherwise quiet store, and Celia reached beneath the counter to pluck the dusty receiver from its chipped and worn cradle. She pressed it to her ear but said nothing. If she hadn't already known who it was, she would have been able to tell from the sound of labored breathing on the other end. The breathing continued for several seconds before the caller finally spoke.

"Celia? Is that you? You there?"

The words were pronounced through an Italian accent that replaced the sound 'th' made at the beginning of a word with a 'd'. Celia smiled and let the man on the other end twist in the wind for a few more seconds.

"Hello? Celia, is that you? *Marone*, this old fucking thing! Hello!?!"

"I'm here, Sal," Celia said flatly, not letting her tone betray the enjoyment she got from the caller's frustration. "You know I'm here."

"Celia, for Christ's sake," said Sal, the anger slowly melting from his tone. "I don't know how they answer a phone where you come from, but here—"

"What do you want, Sal," Celia interrupted.

She was only halfway listening while absently flipping through her magazine. She knew what the man wanted. She always knew.

Sal cleared his throat on the other end of the call, trying to downplay his anger over the curt, flippant way Celia spoke to him. Nobody talked to Sal like that, and *nobody* interrupted him. The lack of respect enraged him, but he didn't dare let it show through the cheery disposition he was fighting to keep up. He knew better.

"I . . . uh, I was calling to check on that thing. I wanted to make sure it was delivered on time and was . . . satisfactory."

She hated the way he spoke in such a vague and roundabout way, but he'd been doing it too long to break the habit now. He was referring to Johnny and wanted to know if the boy was enough to repay his debt. Sal had kept his word, but Celia waited longer than necessary to reply to make him sweat.

"Yes, Sal," she said through the half-smile Johnny used to think was 'so cute'. "I'm satisfied."

Celia hung the phone up, knowing Sal would continue to talk until the dial tone kicked in, but he wouldn't call back. At least, not until the next time he needed something from her.

It had been so long since Celia had the freedom to move, let alone draw from the staggering amount of power she possessed. She was still settling in but took great satisfaction in her short work on the neighborhood hierarchy. It proved she hadn't lost a step but was smart enough to proceed cautiously.

There was no use in blowing her cover just yet, and with Adria dead, there was no one to tether Celia or dictate her every move. The old woman's greed had been her undoing, and Sal was headed in the same direction. It was only a matter of time before he would also belong to Celia, and the rest would fall like dominos.

It may take a while, but the wait would be nothing compared to the time she'd spent locked away in cosmic captivity. Celia smiled and flipped the page of her magazine. Soon, the world would be her playground again, and this time, no one was left on this plane of existence to stop her. ☠

I LIKES 'EM TRASHY

I've always liked my women a little on the trashy side. The ones with elaborate, unnecessary makeup, high boots with short skirts, and piercing eyes glaring through dramatically cut Betty Page bangs. Throw in a few tattoos for good measure, and I'm a happy man. Naturally, I included this information when I signed up for the three-way app Thrinder. I was surprised by the quick response shortly after posting my profile, but I went with it.

The message I received said to meet at a bar called The Tri-Corner Hat for drinks and conversation before getting to business. The couple's names were Greg and Terry, and according to our correspondence, they were 'very excited to meet me'.

When I walked in, I was thrown off by the near-total darkness of the place, but I figured when you're hashing out a threesome with people you met online, it's better to work under cover of darkness. I recognized Greg wearing the same ratty, black ball cap pulled down over the eyes he wore in his picture, sitting at the bar sipping a drink.

"Hey there," I said, walking up to the bar. "Greg, I take it?"

"Oh yeah," he said, smiling wide. "That's me. You must be Larry."

"Guilty as charged," I answered, immediately regretting my corny quip. "Nice to meet you. Is Terry here somewhere?"

"No, actually she's not," he said. "She likes me to meet the person first to make sure it's a . . . good fit for us. You understand?"

"Oh yeah, man," I said. "Totally."

"So," said Greg, "you like 'em trashy, huh?"

"That's right," I said, trying to be as casual as possible. "That's just always been my type."

"Well, you're gonna' love Terry. She's as trashy as they come."

"Sounds great," I replied. "So, when do I get to meet her?"

"Soon," he said. "First, I must ask if you're cool with some kinky shit?"

I'd had my fair share of interesting sexual encounters and felt I could answer confidently.

"Oh yeah, man," I said, leaning into him, "the kinkier the better."

I didn't have a proclivity for kink, but I wanted to set him at ease and get the show on the road. I was excited but didn't want to waste my whole night.

"That's good," he said, "real good. Terry and I get a little weird sometimes if you know what I mean?"

"I sure do," I said, elbowing him playfully in the ribs even though I had no idea what he meant. "I'm down with the get down." That is another cheesy line I regretted.

"Fuck it then," said Greg slamming his drink. "Let's get out of here."

I followed him out of the bar and turned toward the street, but Greg grabbed my shoulder and spun me around.

"It's this way," he said, pointing down the alley between the bar and the abandoned building beside it.

"Oh, uh, okay," I said, following him into the darkness.

"Terry's gonna' be so jazzed to meet you, man. We've been looking for someone who clicks with us, and I have a good feeling about you."

"I aims to please," I said, seemingly unable to not speak in groan-worthy retorts.

The alley was typical as far as alleys go. Bare brick walls lined either side, and piles of garbage sat atop mystery puddles of trash water.

"So where are we going anyway?"

"To meet up with Terry," said Greg without looking back at me. "You wanna' go meet Terry, right?"

"Of course," I said. "Just curious, that's all."

"It's not much farther."

Ahead, I could see a dumpster with light peeking out from the other side of it, and the closer we got, the more I began to hear voices. The light came from a trash barrel fire, and the voices belonged to two bums warming themselves around it. They stopped mid-sentence to gawk as we passed.

"Hey there," said one of them. "You going to see Terry?"

The grizzled bum smiled, revealing a single black tooth while awkwardly rubbing his crotch and licking his scab-covered lips.

"I bet he is," said the other bum, whose tooth count doubled that of his counterpart. "He's got that look."

They laughed and rubbed themselves, the bulges in their pants reacting to the stimulus.

"Shut up, you degenerates," spat Greg. "Why don't you two go fuck yourselves!"

"Sounds good to me," said the first bum as he reached over with his free hand to grab his friend's face and guide it to his own. Their sloppy make-out session sounded like the kneading of wet dough.

"Don't mind them. They don't know shit," said Greg pointing to a door up ahead. "Almost there."

I nodded and sped up to be next to him.

"So, what's Terry like?" I asked. "I mean, you haven't really told me too much."

"What's to tell?" he answered. "She's extra trashy, just like you like 'em, she's into freaky shit, and she's down to fuck. What else do you wanna know?"

"Uh . . . well, I guess that's good enough for me."

The amount of trash lining the alley was stacked over five feet high in some places, and the smell was unbearable. Greg grabbed at the lever on the door and turned to face me.

"You ready?"

"Oh yeah," I said, more ready to get out of the smothering trash than anything else.

The hinges screeched like a cat dragged by a city bus, and I guessed it hadn't been oiled since its installation. Greg stepped in, hit a switch on the wall to his left, and a single light crackled to life from the ceiling in the center of the room, which was completely empty save for a giant pile of trash bags. Greg crossed his arms and smiled, staring at the mound.

"What is this?" I asked.

"That's Terry," he said, pointing to the pile. "Ain't she a beaut?"

I scanned the room to make sure I wasn't missing something.

"A beaut? She's a pile of trash."

"Exactly," he said. "You like 'em trashy, don't ya'?"

"Yeah, but . . . "

Greg walked to the pile. He called Terry, and I followed. The smell was worse than in the alley, and I could see most of the bags were ripped, spilling rotten food, used diapers, and other unidentifiable greasy trash innards.

"What are you waiting for?" asked Greg. "Let's do this!"

He dropped his pants, exposing his very erect, very large penis, which he promptly buried into the side of Terry. I'm not sure what came over me, but I was instantly aroused and, not wanting to be outdone, dropped my pants to show off my considerable endowment as well.

"Now we're talking," said Greg. "Get on in there. She's nice and wet."

Before I knew it, I was humping along with Greg at a furious pace. I groped at lumps of wet garbage that came away in my hand as I tried to find purchase on top of Terry. I rolled around her, sticking myself into any opening I could find, each one wet with anticipation. I was so engrossed in what I was doing that I forgot about Greg until I heard him cry.

"Oh man, oh man," he called from the other side of Terry, where he was thrusting away with reckless abandon. "I'm gonna' cum!"

I eased up and repositioned myself thinking it was kind of soon for him to already be cumming, but I wasn't going to say anything.

"Oh yeah, baby. Oh yeah, baby," he said, panting into climax. "Oh yeeeaaahhhh!"

Greg shook with the intensity of his orgasm, savoring every last quake. He threw his head back, and his cap fell to the floor behind him. Something was wrong, but I didn't want to believe what I was seeing. The top of Greg's head was a garbage bag with bits of paper, coffee grinds, and other trash spilling from it.

"What the—,"

That was all I could muster before Greg's face fell off, and more trash spilled out from behind it. I watched in disbelief, still pumping away, as his body fell apart in front of me, revealing lumpy, leaking bags of trash that fell into Terry, becoming part of her.

I was shocked, but I did come here to fuck, so I pounded away until I was finished. I stepped away from Terry, zipped up, and took one final look around. I walked over to where Greg had been to find all that was left of him was his hat. I picked up the dirty, black thing, dusted it off, and put it on, pulling the brim down firmly over my eyes. I walked to a large steel door, opened it, and looked at the trash pile.

"Thanks, Terry," I said. "It was fun. Maybe I'll see you around sometime." ☠

TRENCHMAN

Carrie peered through the curtains of her bedroom window. He was still there. She didn't know why she expected anything different since he'd been standing on the sidewalk across the street from her house for the last five days. Every time she looked out, he would hold up his hand, displaying a finger for each day he'd been there.

His trench coat plunged to the ground, completely covering his feet. The oversized collar was popped and pulled close to his face, obscuring his features. Dark eyes shining like polished onyx were the only thing visible through the shadows.

Carrie referred to him as Trenchman.

Since his arrival, things had gotten strange around the neighborhood, and while she knew him to be directly responsible, she didn't know how since all he did was stand across the street all day and all night.

First, the power had gone out, followed by cellular and landline phone service, making the Internet completely inaccessible. Carrie had no way to contact anyone, and nobody could reach her. Her parents were gone, having become the first victims of Trenchman on the second day he'd been there. She'd pointed out to her parents the man standing across the street staring at her window for the last two days, and her father strutted to confront him. Her mother watched from the lawn, Carrie from the window.

Her father approached the man to engage politely, his chosen way of handling confrontation, and Trenchman responded by reaching out and pulling her father's face off. He didn't *rip* it off like in the bloody gore-filled horror movies she'd seen, but instead simply grabbed the skin below her father's chin and peeled it away like removing a bandage.

Trenchman opened his coat just enough to slip her father's face inside while his body swayed dazedly before collapsing on the sidewalk a second later. Carrie's mother screamed, dashed across the street, and knelt next to her fallen husband a moment before standing to face Trenchman.

She'd barely gotten a word out when he grabbed her face in the same manner, peeled it away, and slipped it into his coat. Carrie watched her mother's body wobble like a toy whose battery was dying before she collapsed.

That was only the second day, though. On the fifth day, bodies piled up on the sidewalk around Trenchman since anyone who approached him met the same fate as Carrie's parents. She watched from her window as he removed the faces of her neighbors, the mailman, random passersby, and even a few police officers unable to call for backup since their radios stopped working along with everything else. Trenchman peeled faces off one by one with no noticeable effort and added them to the collection in his coat.

Carrie sat at her window the entire fifth-day watching Trenchman while Trenchman watched her back. They watched each other until the sun began to rise, and Trenchman held up all five fingers of his left hand and one from his right hand beside it. Carrie knew what would happen next and stepped back from the window. During the fifth day, nobody approached Trenchman, the only day such a thing had happened since her father started it off.

No one else was coming, and Carrie knew it; now it was her turn. She was the only one left to face Trenchman and had already resigned herself to the same fate as the others. She figured being faceless and dead was better than being alone forever.

Carrie slipped on the winter coat she kept hung by the front door. It hadn't seen much use in the last week, and this was probably its last hurrah. She stepped into her boots and pulled the fur lining of her hood close to her face to smell it one last time before stepping outside.

The piles of bodies looked much different from this vantage point and seemed like they'd gotten impossibly bigger. Thin wafts of steam rose steadily from the banks, which she hadn't noticed from her window's view. There was the smell too, or rather the lack thereof. Carrie thought this many dead bodies would produce an overpowering, heinous stench, but she smelled nothing save the crispness in the winter air.

There was a clear path directly from Carrie's front door to Trenchman, which she'd known was by design. The collar still hid his face, but behind it, the floating black orbs stayed trained on her, and she pulled her coat tightly against her body as she began the walk. Trenchman stood frozen with the only movement coming from his chest's steady rise and fall as he breathed calm and even. She studied the bodies as she passed by who were all faceless, only instead of bloody exposed skulls, there was blank, featureless flesh running smooth and flat across the space their faces used to occupy.

Carrie stepped up to Trenchman, confidently staring into the black eyes of his shadowed face. Several seconds of silence passed between the two, and she detected a slight change in his eyes that made her think he was smiling.

"You made it six whole days," said Trenchman, finally breaking the silence.

"Yeah," said Carrie, unsure if he even expected her to answer.

"Too bad, I can do that standing on my head." With that, he reached out and tapped her on the shoulder. "You're it! Oh, and good luck beating twenty-seven faces!"

"What?" Carrie was talking to no one, though. Trenchman had run past her, down the path, and into the house. The door slammed behind him.

Carrie stood puzzled momentarily and stared at the house as if she expected it to explain what had just happened. Suddenly, up in the window, *her* window appeared the head of Trenchman. He pulled down his collar to reveal he was actually a little girl, a little girl who looked just like Carrie except for the eyes. The eyes remained as black and ominous as they'd always been.

The icy wind blew, and Carrie pulled the coat to her body even tighter, only it wasn't her coat anymore. Now, she was wearing an oversized trench coat that scraped the ground at her feet. The wind launched another chilling attack, and Carrie pulled the collar up to protect her face and neck. She looked to the window again, and the little girl smiled, waved, and held a finger. Carrie mimicked the action back. Day one had begun.

Six days was a long time. It was probably the longest Carrie had ever lasted, and she cursed herself for not being stronger. Suddenly, she heard someone call to her. She turned to see a man approaching from up the sidewalk, weaving in and out of the bodies without giving it a second thought.

"Hey, buddy," the man said. "What are you doing here? You can't be here. You understand me?"

Carried sighed, and when the man was within arm's reach, she grabbed the skin beneath his chin and peeled. ☠

COMPARTMENTS

ompartments. That's all that's left of this place anymore, really. Gone are the streets and sidewalks we used to use to get from one place to another. First the buildings stared edging out slightly taking more and more of the sidewalks until one day they were just gone. It was like they never existed at all. We adapted, of course, but then the streets stared getting narrow. Four lane highways were halved overnight, and two-lane city avenues, streets and drives became one single lane with no instruction as to which way you were to proceed. There were many accidents, and a lot of good people died, but a lot of good people usually must die in the wake of great change.

The accidents and confusion stopped a day later, because by the time the sun came up again the lanes were far too narrow for cars to fit through anymore. The fearless traveled by bike or on foot for the next hour or so until the build out was complete, and just like that, roads were gone altogether. Compartments were all that was left. A few of the more stubborn pedestrians allowed themselves to be crushed between buildings hoping to achieve martyrdom, but nobody noticed they were gone. Besides, dying for a cause had gone out of fashion years ago, and these days nobody gave a shit about causes.

I imagine the overwhelming apathetic malaise, which we found ourselves deeply embroiled in constantly helped facilitate the change, but I don't really care. Nobody else does either. It's business as usual these days; only all business has been compartmentalized along with everything else. The entire city is packed miles across in all directions with compartments stacked more than a hundred stories high. The bustling energy from the millions of people and cars constantly moving about has been replaced by the near-silent shuffling of compartments shifting through the infrastructure like one giant game of Tetris.

My compartment is agreeable to me. It's not very big, but it's not as small as it could be either. It's comfortable enough, and I don't even remember the things that used to bother me about it anymore, but I guess I can chalk that up to the apathy I mentioned earlier. One good thing about the compartments is that we no longer have to interact physically with people, or at least *I* think that's a good thing. The horribly awkward chitchat, handshaking, and eye contact were gone all thanks to compartments. The only way you ever saw another person these days was on the flat fifteen-inch com-screen mounted in the wall, and even then, it was only people you worked with.

Today I woke up as my compartment began to slowly shift and move among its countless counterparts signaling that the workday was close to beginning. The movement was so fluid and quiet it was almost imperceptible, but I could always feel the first movement of the day. I worked for the Valray Corporation, and every morning the compartments of everyone who worked there slid together to form the Valray Block.

We would work the day away until all at once each compartment would disengage from the Block, and slither through the city maze back to its designated spot. I used to wonder why the compartments even had to move since it wasn't like we would know the difference between one place and another, but there must have been an important reason, which was none of my concern.

I pulled on the same white slacks and shirt I wore every day to work just as the Valray logo appeared on my screen signaling that the workday was about to begin. I took a seat at the small desk situated below my screen and the Valray logo was replaced by an image of Mr. Valray, himself.

"Good morning, sir," I said to the screen knowing full well that he couldn't see or hear me.

"Good morning, everyone," said Mr. Valray addressing the entire Block. He was a round-faced, balding man, with a moustache that drooped off in thin wisps of hair like the ones desperately clinging to life atop his head. "Your assignments are being sent out now. Let's work hard and have a great day! Thanks everyone."

Mr. Valray's face flickered away and was replaced by the logo once again. The soft buzz of the printer signaled the arrival of my assignment, and I ripped it from the tray anxious to begin. I scanned it just to make sure nothing was out of the ordinary and placed it on the corner of my desk for reference. My job never really changed from day to day. All I did was receive documents through a transfer tube, sign off that I had inspected them, and send them off to their next destination.

I don't know where that was, or even what the documents were referencing. I just knew to check the designated spots to make sure they had been populated with information, and if they were, I stamped them with my seal and sent them on their way.

Just as the first document of the day landed on the desk, my screen crackled to life again, and Denise was staring down at me. Denise was a co-worker whose compartment was situated next to mine, or at least that's what she told me. I had no way of knowing for sure. Denise was a fair-skinned ginger who no longer had to worry about being burned by a sun she'd never see again. She had chubby cheeks that I guessed were a byproduct of her incessant smiling. I never saw her not smiling when she appeared on my screen ever, and I found it mildly off-putting.

"Good morning you," she said through a toothy smile, of course. She was sending a two-way transmission so only us could see and hear each other. Chatting with me seemed to be her favorite pastime, and while I didn't mind it sometimes; I mostly found it annoying and counterproductive.

"Good morning, Denise," I said allowing my eyes to flutter up and meet hers for only a second before returning back to my work.

"Oh man," she continued, "did you see Mr. Valray's moustache this morning? It looks so creepy! When is he gonna' give that thing up?"

"Yup," I said monotone. "Who knows?"

Denise always had something negative to say about Mr. Valray, and while I recognized it as her way of starting a conversation, I still found it disrespectful.

"Are you already working? Boy, what a go-getter you are. I haven't even pulled my assignment sheet yet. What, are you trying to kiss-up to Valray or something?"

Her tone was such that she was clearly joking, but I took offense, nonetheless. It wasn't that I couldn't take a joke, but the fact that it was the same joke daily got under my skin.

"Yup," I grunted. "I suppose so."

She took the hint that I wasn't into making small talk, and reluctantly ended the conversation.

"Okay, well . . . I guess I'll get to it myself. Can't have you showing me up now, can I?"

I nodded slightly without looking up, and a moment later Denise's face was replaced by the Valray logo. Maybe it was Denise's constant positive attitude that got under my skin, or maybe I felt violated by her incessant intrusions into my compartment. The intrusions were in video form via com-screen but intrusions, nonetheless. I buried my head in work and temporarily forgot how much Denise annoyed me.

Soft music crept from the speakers built into the corners of my compartment and swirled around without me realizing for the first few minutes. Once I became conscious of it, I reached out for the knob on the side of my desk that controlled the volume and turned it all the way down. Valray provided a wide selection of music for its employees to listen to while they worked, but I preferred silence to the soothing sounds of the string quartet currently playing.

The main reason being this was the only music I could get to play in my compartment. The knob that toggled between the styles and genres available stopped working weeks ago. I put a repair request in with the maintenance department, but it still hadn't been fixed since it was a *low priority* issue. It wouldn't be all that bad, except the song never changed. As soon as it ended, it would start right back up from the beginning again.

I never pay much attention to the time while I'm working, but it felt like a couple of hours must have gone by when I heard it again. The soft sound of two violins, a viola, and a cello blending seamlessly into one swelled from behind and snuffed out the precious silence. My hand shot to the volume knob and cranked it back to zero. I made a note to update my maintenance request, so it included this new issue with the volume and went back to my work. I started scanning over a new report when my com-screen flickered, and I found myself once again face to face with Denise.

"Hey there," she said through the beaming smile I'd come to loathe. "Working hard, or hardly working? Ha ha, just kidding! I know you're always working."

Denise used this joke often whenever she wanted to shoehorn her way into my day at random. I suppose she thought her 'humor' somehow made her intrusions acceptable, but I found them appalling regardless. I glanced up for just a moment, as per usual, and gave a half grunt with a nod in response.

"Anywho," she continued, "are you having any issues with the music in your compartment? Mine is kind of acting weird."

This caught my attention enough to pull me from my state of actively ignoring Denise.

"Yeah, I mean yes," I said cursing myself for allowing genuine emotion to show through in my reply. "It has been . . . malfunctioning lately. I've already put a maintenance request in though. If yours is acting up, I suggest you do the same."

I slammed my eyes back down to the work on my desk intent on not looking up at the screen again. As far as I was concerned, the conversation was over. She asked her question, and I answered it. Unfortunately, Denise didn't see it that way, and continued to talk.

"Mine has been stuck on one station for a while," she said, "and the volume has been changing without me even touching it."

"Yeah, well like I said," I spat snapping my eyes back up to the com-screen, "you should submit a maintenance re—"

I stopped short unsure of what I had seen. Surely, it was a glitch in the com-screen. Denise had an annoying habit of putting her face right up to the camera so all you could see of her was from the chin up, but just now I thought I'd caught a glimpse of her neck for the first time. It looked like she was wearing a necklace, and I had no reason to believe it was anything but that, however, something seemed odd. Maybe it was because I was seeing something of Denise other than just her irritating chubby face that took me aback, or maybe I had good reason to feel uneasy.

The necklace appeared to be made of tiny sharp teeth no bigger than those of a cat. It wasn't just the teeth that struck me as odd; it was that there was so many of them, rows upon rows. More disconcerting was the skin around Denise's neck. It was red, irritated, and looked torn in some places. The glimpse I caught was so short; I decided the unsavoriness of what I thought I saw was a product of my own imagination.

"Yeah, I suppose that's what I should do," said Denise's face from the com-screen. Her neck wasn't visible. Maybe it never had been. "I might leave it alone for a while though. I kind of like this song."

I heard the familiar whine of violin strings, and my hand instinctively shot out to twist the volume back to zero. The knob was already turned down though, and I realized the music was coming through the speaker of my com-screen.

"That's the same song that's been playing in my compartment for weeks," I said. "What even is that?"

"Do you like it too?" Asked Denise. "It's Bela Bartok's *An Expression of Unrequited Love* in four movements. He wrote it when he fell in love with a young violinist virtuoso named Stefi Geyer and found she didn't reciprocate the feeling."

"God no," I said trying to sound as disgusted as possible "No wonder she didn't love him back if this is the kind of uninspired drivel he wrote."

I didn't really feel this way about the piece and found it quite soothing and enjoyable particularly when I was going to sleep, but my disdain for Denise would not allow me to have an actual conversation with her in which we discussed our tastes in music.

"Oh, really?" Asked Denise. The tone of her voice slightly shifted to that of disappointment, and while I felt a tinge of guilt for blowing her off, I suppressed it and nodded emphatically.

"Yes, yes I do," I said. "I'd rather listen to Mr. Valray recite the company handbook on proper procedure than listen to that song one more time."

"Yeah," sighed Denise, "me too, I guess. I'm going to put in my maintenance request right now. See you later."

Denise's face was gone from my screen and replaced by the bouncing Valray logo. I put her out of my mind and lost myself in my job. I lived for the work. I often wished my compartment never had to disembark from the Valray Block, and I'd only just recently worked up the courage to outline a proposal on why my never leaving would be beneficial *and* profitable to the company. I had no idea when I'd have the balls to actually present it to Mr. Valray himself, but I would do it eventually.

The familiar opening notes of Bartok's temper tantrum of a love song in four movements broke my focus, and I inadvertently crumpled the edges of the document I was holding. As if on cue, the fat gingery face of Denise popped onto my com-screen accompanied by her high-pitched squawk ripping through the tiny speaker.

"Oh my god," she sang happily. "Did the song just come on in your compartment? The song just came on in mine! Oh my god, I hear it! It *is* playing in your compartment at the same time! Oh my god! Why do you think that is?"

I slammed the document down hard, and my small desk shook as my hand shot out to twist the volume knob back to zero. I cut my eyes up to meet Denise's and shot fiery hatred through the electronics of the communication system. I know she felt it too, because I saw it. I saw it in her face.

"Denise," I roared, "If you do not stop communicating with me during working hours, I will have no choice but to file a formal complaint against you with Mr. Valray! I do not care if the same music comes on in our compartments, as I do not see how it is relevant to the work we are assigned to complete. As I said before, I suggest you file a maintenance request, and deal with the issue until it can be fixed. Now please, leave me alone."

I snapped my com-screen to the 'one-way' setting, and Denise's face flickered away. I took a deep breath, and methodically smoothed the document I'd wrinkled until my pulse slowed back to a normal pace. As much as I hated being overcome with emotion, in this instance it was necessary. Maybe now I would finally be rid of her annoying and pointless interruptions for good. I inspected the crumpled paper and smoothed it out one last time before sending it on its next stop hoping I wouldn't receive any demerits for its poor condition.

That's when I heard it. At first, I thought it was the music again, only the sound wasn't coming from the speakers but from outside my compartment. What started as a soft steady tapping grew to a loud banging, and then a full-on pounding. I sat frozen staring at a spot on the wall to my left that was beginning to bow out and crack under the force of what was pressing from behind.

I was completely unprepared and didn't know the correct protocol for this situation. I'm sure there was something I was supposed to do, but I didn't know what it was. To the left of my com-screen was a small shelf that housed the essential literature on Valray policy and procedure, and I quickly scanned the spines looking for one that dealt with emergency situations. I reached out to grab the manual, but just as I did all the manuals fell from the shelf as my entire compartment shook from the final breaching blow.

Panic seized me as I crashed to the floor along with the Valray literature and several other items in my compartment. I looked up to see there was indeed a hole in the wall. It was only slightly larger than the size of a quarter, but a hole nonetheless, and I curled into a ball with my hands over my head. The pounding stopped but I wasn't about to let my guard down, so I stayed on the floor, my eyes shut tight waiting for the other shoe to drop. After several seconds of silence, Bartok's familiar composition began to circulate around the otherwise silent space of my compartment.

The music wasn't coming from my speakers this time though; it was coming through the small hole in the wall. I opened my eyes, uncovered my head and looked around to see my com-screen displaying an extra-smiley Denise.

"Hey, you," she sung from the screen. "What are you doing down there on the floor silly? Get up."

I pulled myself up with my desk and looked Denise right in her blubbery, smiling face.

"Something happened," I said shakily. "Something—something just broke through the wall of my compartment. Did you feel anything? Do you know—."

I glanced at my com-screen controls and saw it was still switched to 'one-way' communication, and Denise shouldn't be able contact me like this. She noticed me staring dumbfounded as *An Expression of Unrequited Love* grew louder coming now from my speakers as well as through the hole.

"I know you're probably confused," said Denise, "but don't worry. I've had control of your compartment for . . . sheesh, quite a while now."

"Wait. What—" I stood so I was eyelevel with my com-screen. "You mean you've been doing—*this*? And that?"

I pointed to the hole in my wall looking back and forth from it to the screen.

"Oh, don't act so surprised," said Denise giggling. "You've had to have known it was me. I've been dropping hints for months."

"Hints? Hints about what?"

"About how I feel about you silly," she continued. "I know you can be, well, sort of aloof especially when you're working. That's why I had to step up my game."

"Game?" I asked perplexed still unsure of what was going on.

"Yeah, my 'game'. That's why I started playing the song over and over for you. That's why I had to break through. I had to get to you. I have something for you."

I approached the hole to better inspect the damage. "Are you on the other side of this?"

"Well, of course I am," she said. "I told you we were right next to each other. Now, like I said, I have something for you."

I got closer and saw something pushing through the opening. It was small, dripping with shiny dark slime, and black as I had ever seen black be. The thing slid past the breach coating its path in sludge, and I could see it was resting on the end of a long wooden spoon. I thought it was a badly burned acorn attached to thin gold chain, but when I took a closer look, I saw it was pulsing. Small pockets of the dark ooze worked their way out of jaggedly torn holes in the thing with every pulse.

"What is this?"

I looked back to Denise's face on the screen, but all she did was smile.

"It's my heart," she said tearing up. "I've been in love with you since the first time I accidentally com-screened you back when I joined the block. You were different from everyone else I'd ever had the chance to talk to, and I knew we had to be together. That's why I want you to have my heart. I put a chain on it so you can wear it for always. It belongs to you now, but I like to think it always did."

I turned back to the hole and realized the burned acorn was actually a tiny, beating, black heart. I fought the urge to react emotionally and paused to collect my thoughts.

"Denise," I started. "I think we should contact Valray emergency services and get you some help. You're clearly not well, and it would be in your best interest to get someone down here to help you. Now, Valray has an excellent medical and psychological team that can—"

"Emergency services?" Denise half asked, half screamed at me. "I'm not sick you idiot, I'm in love! I'm in love with you! I'm trying to give you my heart, and here you are treating me like I'm physically and mentally unstable? You're no better than that little bitch violinist who threw Bartok's love back in his face!"

My compartment shook, and I held the desk tight to keep from losing my balance. Denise's smile was replaced by a scowl and the entire dynamic of her facial structure transformed into something dark and sinister. The heart began to retreat back through the hole, and the compartment rocked again knocking me from my feet.

"Denise," I called out, "please stop this. I'm sorry. We can get you help, but whatever you're doing please stop."

"You're sorry?" Her voice changed to match her face. Gone was the saccharine drenched lilt replaced by something that sounded like her vocal cords had been hacked at by white-hot cleavers. "Well, I'm sorry too! I tried to be nice to you, I tried to let you know how I felt, I tried to give you my heart. Now, I'm going to give you my curse!"

Denise stepped back from her com-screen camera to reveal herself from the neck down to me for the first time. I wouldn't believe it if I weren't seeing it. It turned out I hadn't imagined the odd necklace of teeth earlier, only it wasn't a necklace. Denise backed up against the far wall of her compartment, and I stood with my face close to the com-screen for a better look. I wish I hadn't.

Thousands and thousands of the tiny, sharp, cat-toothy things were wrapped around her body like a demonic hose on a human spool. The teeth were all connected but there were so many I couldn't tell until they started to move. The thing began to slink away from her feet across the room, and as it unwound, I saw what Denise meant by curse. The flesh beneath the slithering, tubular, teeth-monster was all but gone save for a few jiggling chunks of muscle with dangling twitchy ligaments. The remnants stood out against the bright white bone that was otherwise picked clean. The creature continued slithering down further revealing more and more of the grotesque horror show left in its wake.

Soon I was staring at a blood-splotched skeleton with the untouched head of Denise balanced atop the tower of bones, her eyes blasting electronic rays of hate. The creature vanished from the screen, and my heart sunk as I whipped around afraid of what I might see but there it was. Her 'curse' was creeping through the hole

in the wall that just so happened to be a perfect fit, which I guessed wasn't by coincidence.

I turned halfway back to the screen still keeping one eye on the thing and pleaded with Denise.

"Denise, please," I shouted, "I'm sorry, okay! I am so sorry for hurting your feelings. Please, call this—thing off, and let's talk about it. Maybe we can give it a try between us? You know, start slow and see if we're a good fit. Just give me a chance!"

"Give you a chance? I've given you chance, after chance, after chance, so the time for chances is through. Goodbye forever. I hope you have better luck with *this* than I did."

The com-screen went black, and I jumped as the creature came within inches of my feet. It flowed from the hole like it was coming out of a teeth-dispensing soft-serve machine. The thing stopped shy of my big toe, paused for a moment, and started to back up. A glimmer of hope shot through me as I figured Denise had seen the light. She just wanted to scare me, that's all. She was upset that I spurned her advances, and she needed to blow off some steam. I waited for the thing retreat through the hole back into Denise's compartment but that didn't happen.

The monster rose up and began to coil around itself until it was almost as tall as I was. That song had been playing the whole time, and Bartok's masterpiece was approaching the main theme when the creature sprung. The coil widened mid-air to accommodate my frame and I suddenly found myself swallowed by countless hungry grinding teeth.

Hundreds of miniature razors began to tear the skin from my face and body as the musical piece reached its prominent violin solo. I imagine Bartok had written this with his love in mind to play the part, and as blackness overtook the pain, I wept bloody tears over what a beautiful song it truly was. ☠

GROUNDHOG DAY

The cold was bitter and biting like it always was toward the end of January, but it didn't bother me as much as Groundhog Day.

Our family didn't celebrate Groundhog Day in the traditional sense, although there were similarities. While we were concerned with whether or not the groundhog saw its shadow, the prolonging of winter or ushering in of spring were of no consequence to us. Celebrating a rodent's conjured weather forecasting abilities is as foolish as devoting an entire day to honor the thing, a day that served no purpose. Our concern was with Apep and what the groundhog seeing its shadow meant to him regarding us.

There's a hole, or it's more like a pit on my grandfather's property. It's a twenty-acre plot on the outskirts of town where the highway turns into a two-lane road, and it's been in my family for generations. When my grandfather passes, my dad will take it over, and when he's gone, it'll be my responsibility to care for the land and protect our tradition.

The pit used to be out in the open, but when the city began encroaching further north, getting closer to the property, a structure was built around the hole to keep it obscured. The barn, as we took to calling it, had been there since I was born, and my dad said he got to help build it when he was a kid, which was an important point of pride that showed through any time he brought it up.

Every year, our entire family would come in from all over to gather at the property for Groundhog Day, with some arriving as early as New Year's to stay the whole month. They would clean up, make any repairs my grandfather could not do, and take care of all necessary preparations for the big day.

My grandfather lived in a sprawling ranch-style house that had been added onto a few times since I was born, but even more times before. Despite the seemingly constant amendments to the home, it didn't appear cobbled together, and there was plenty of room for the entire family to stay if they wanted.

Of course, you weren't required to arrive early or stay in the house. The only requirement was to be there on February 2nd. If someone didn't show up, whether by choice or not, it was an automatic forfeiture on their part. Only a year ago, I discovered what 'forfeiture' meant and why we never saw those relatives again. We haven't had a family member miss in over ten years, and so far, it looked like we'd make it eleven.

On the morning of Groundhog Day, the family would gather in the barn and stand around the pit silently, listening to the small radio my grandfather held up in the air. Nothing would happen until the official broadcast took place. If it were reported the groundhog did *not* see his shadow, we would all hug and whoop for joy.

Then, we would walk back across the property together to the house for a day of food and celebration, except for my grandfather and father, who would stay back to receive the gift from Apep. The gift wasn't tangible, like money or gold, but was more like luck or a blessing. Dad told me it kept us all safe and prosperous for another year.

If it was announced the groundhog *did* see his shadow, the barn would remain silent, and my grandfather would turn off the radio. The ground would begin to rumble, starting with a slight vibration that built quickly to shake the entire structure.

That was when you would see his eyes, Apep's eyes burning red and gold up from the blackness of the pit. The glowing orbs were hideous and beautiful at the same time, but none of us dared do more than sneak a glance. Any longer wasn't worth it lest you give Apep reason to *select* you.

Once the selection was made, things moved rather quickly. We grew up being told it was indiscriminate, but there was no way to know. There would be a sound like a short burst of air being released from a pressurized tank, and while the one selected would feel it before the rest of us saw it, their screaming would point us in the right direction.

Apep would launch a stream of venom out from the pit, and the person it struck was selected. The viscous poison would burn through their skin, a ghastly fate in and of itself, but the true horror show followed. While the searing pain might make them wish for death, they certainly didn't want it in the way it was to be doled out.

The lengths of pipe and wooden clubs everyone carried would start coming out at this time, and the selected would be beaten savagely before being kicked into the pit. With the messy business finished, we would silently file out and return to the house for a mournful breakfast with no mirth and minimal conversation. There would be no gift, and the year would be dismal for the entire family.

We never speculated on or tried to plan for what having our luck lifted for an entire year would mean since it was no use wasting energy on fighting the inevitable. All we could do was put it from our minds and take each day as it came with the solace of knowing the chance to get our luck back was only a year away.

The family's luck hadn't been revoked for five straight years, and we all hoped to make it six, but I woke up with a bad feeling this morning. I'd been staying in the house on the property the entire week leading up to today, along with my dad and a few of the early arrivers, to help prepare. Every day this week, I'd woken with a belly full of hope and insurmountable optimism, but today was decidedly different. There was no hope, and there was no optimism. There was nothing. I felt nothing at all, and it scared me.

I spent the morning trying to convince myself it was just nerves or anxiety, but as we filed into the barn, the wooden club in my back pocket felt suddenly heavier, like it knew something I didn't. It was exciting. My grandfather brought up the rear and shut and latched the door behind him before taking his place in front of the pit.

He turned on his radio, and I saw several people flinch from the click of the switch alone. It was becoming obvious other family members were feeling the same empty dread, already anticipating bad news. The dial was pre-set to the correct station and needed only minor adjustments to make the broadcast loud and clear.

And we have the best prices guaranteed on our new selection of cu—

An ad for a local appliance store played while the combined anticipation of the family filled the barn with suffocating anxiety. There was a rustle as people shifted their weight from one foot to the other, but their nervous, whispered conversations abruptly halted when my grandfather raised his hand, calling for quiet as the commercial ended.

The broadcaster started by announcing the weather, and according to him, the current temperature was twenty-two degrees Fahrenheit and partly cloudy with a seventy percent chance of rain. He added that the wind-chill factor made the twenty-two degrees feel negative seven.

We hadn't had a cold winter in over five years, and I caught a shiver from the wind whipping through gaps between the old wooden slats of the barn's east wall. The fact it was an east wind made for a bad omen, but I put the thought from my mind and focused on the broadcast.

The announcement was made so casually that it took me a moment to grasp what I'd heard. It took most of the family by surprise, too, and you could feel the answer ripple through the tension in the room.

—with a final score of 88 to 87 after one overtime period. Don't put away your winter coat just yet because word out of Pennsylvania this morning is to expect six more weeks of winter. That's right, folks. Today is February 2nd, Groundhog Day, and the mayor of Punxsutawney gave the official report moments ago that the groundhog has indeed seen his shadow! In other news, the market has tak—

My grandfather turned the radio off, and this time, the click resonated as a signal of the end. The end of the family's luck for the next year and the end of someone's life. I didn't realize I'd been staring into the pit until the eyes started to glow. People were shuffling nervously around me, and I looked from the pit to my grandfather to see he was staring down at the eyes and holding the small radio against his chest.

The ground started to shake, and the entire family held their breath as they waited for someone to be chosen. I was sure I would see it when I heard the rush of air, but I blinked and missed it. Then, the screaming started. The cries came from my left and belonged to my father. The sound he made seemed so foreign coming from his mouth, like the high-pitched wail of a eunuch, and if I hadn't been able to see it, I wouldn't have believed it was him.

A club rose over his head from behind, attached to the hand of one of my first cousins, but before he could strike, my father dropped to his knees out of the way. The errant blow came down on the shoulder of an aunt whom I knew by face, not name, and she wailed like a dying cat as she crumpled to the ground.

This seemed to confuse everyone for a moment, long enough for my father to have crawled through the tangle of legs to the back of the barn. I swiveled my head around just as he popped up, pushed a pipe-wielding uncle hard to the ground, and hit the door. The earth shook violently as he broke the threshold of the barn and sprinted out across the field.

Chaos spread like fire through a leaf pile, and within seconds, cries of confusion turned to screams of anger as family members pushed through the open door, chasing after my father, the selected. I saw my grandfather trying to get everyone's attention, but he couldn't be heard over the co-mingled shouts of the family.

Cousins and nephews brushed past to join the chase, nearly knocking me, but I held my ground and watched as my grandfather turned to face the pit. A giant, six-armed cobra rose from the darkness and towered over the remaining family members in the barn.

It happened so quickly; if I hadn't seen my grandfather's legs dangling from the serpent's mouth a moment before being sucked down its expanding throat, I would have thought he just vanished. I watched the man-shaped bulge slide down into the snake as a cross between a roar and a hiss erupted from the great Apep's open, unhinged maw. Large drops of saliva-diluted venom rained down on those left, scrambling to get out as the dynamic suddenly changed from pursuing to being pursued.

I was fortunate not to have been struck by the acidic saliva on my bare skin, but a few drops hit the front of my shirt, which I quickly shed once contact was made. The garment hissed and smoldered on the ground at my feet while the toxic substance ate through the fabric, turning it into a pile of rags.

I'd only ever heard stories about what Apep looked like, but seeing the serpent deity's hypnotic visage for myself left me awestruck. Two fangs like sabers jutted menacingly from the monstrous mouth while rows of smaller teeth equally as sharp filled the remaining available space. Three humanoid muscle-bound arms extended from both sides of the giant cobra just below its hood with curved, black, razor talons attached to claw hands.

Green and gold scales ran up and down the snake-God, radiating a shimmering, otherworldly glow. I didn't realize I'd been backing away from the pit until I tripped over the body of an unrecognizable family member whose face hung melted from a bare and grinning skull.

As the creature struck, I rolled out of the way, and he snatched the unknown family member instead. Apep bit down, spraying blood from his mouth as I scrambled and sprinted for the door. The unique deafening roar chased me from the barn, but I didn't stop to turn around even when I heard the first explosion.

Outside, most family members ran for their lives while others stopped completely, facing the direction of the barn with fixed expressions of terror. Some pointed while others clutched at their chests, bawling. I heard a second tremendous crash and couldn't help glancing back this time.

Apep had grown even larger and ripped through the old barn's roof, which was responsible for the first explosion. The second came when he crashed through the structure, knocking out an entire wall as he slithered across the open field chasing after my fleeing family. The three remaining walls sagged inward from lack of support, and it wouldn't be long before they collapsed.

About thirty yards ahead, I saw a small cluster of five or six family members gathered around something on the ground, which now turned their attention to the fast-approaching Apep. I tried to yell for them to run but was breathing too hard for words to come out. I glimpsed the ground as I blew by and saw my father's bloodied and brutally beaten body. The venom and the administered beating drastically altered his appearance, but I could tell it was him.

The thought of stopping vanished as quickly as it had come on, and I continued to run. I could do nothing for him now, and mourning the loss of his life would have to be dealt with when I wasn't currently trying to save my own.

"Oh, great and powerful, Apep," I heard behind me. "We have caught the selected who tried to flee your gr—"

They were cut off by their own screams, followed by the distinct sound of snapping bones as Apep showed his 'appreciation' by devouring them. The attempt to appease the ancient one was apparently too little, too late, and I didn't know how or if we could stop him. I was starting to catch up to the rest of the runners, who were slowing down now, gasping to breathe the frosty air as they struggled to keep moving.

I passed them quickly, forcing myself to ignore their screams of terror as they were picked off one by one by their own God. My cousin Albert was the only person still in front of me, but he looked over his shoulder and tripped, nearly taking me down with him. Luckily, I could leap over his tumbling form without breaking stride.

I was almost to the house, but I didn't know what to do once I got there. Maybe Apep would stay focused on the remaining family in the field and forget all about me? Perhaps I could get the keys to my grandfather's truck and use it to make a real break for it? Maybe I could ge—

My point of view changed suddenly as I realized I was now moving away from the house. I should have felt my back-breaking and knee bends the wrong way, but either Apep's venom numbed me, or the shock switched off my pain receptors. As the mighty serpent lifted me, I saw its massive, sprawling shadow cast darkness across the property. I'd had a feeling we were due for a bad year, but not to this extent.

I started to feel sleepy, and the thought of a bad year didn't bother me as much anymore as the moist, warm confines of Apeps's mouth went from terrifying to comforting. I closed my eyes, and all my thoughts evaporated as I felt the gentle expanding and contracting of Apep's muscles push me slowly down his throat. ☠

CURSE OF THE WENDIGO

Mark stole money from his mom's purse without being caught. It was easy stuff, no sweat, but this was different. He wasn't stealing cash conveniently located in his mother's wallet; he was stealing a silver bowl and taking it from a church, technically stealing from God, but he was pretty sure it wasn't a mortal sin.

Rich would be back in the woods waiting for him by now, and Mark needed to get to the clearing pronto. He'd been waiting long enough, and it was time to move. He rose slowly from behind the pew, stepping carefully to avoid the floorboards he knew creaked, allowing him to glide up the aisle to the pulpit with the silent grace of a vampire.

He remembered not too long ago, he would have found the analogy cool, but his present reality made it a terrifying thought.

Neither of the boys thought it would be *this* serious. Their minds were pre-programmed by movies. Holly Wood's polished spin on all things supernatural may depict some extreme circumstances, but in the end, a resolution was waiting to wrap it all up with a bow on top.

You still feel finality even when they throw an unexpected twist to set up a sequel. Sequels usually involve a different cast except for a holdover or two, which is rare nowadays. Rich and Mark failed to grasp the reality of what they'd done, viewing it more as a game to be put back on the shelf when they were bored and not a frightening mess that had the potential to never end.

Things got out of hand before they'd even started. Mark wanted to blame Rich since he'd made the suggestion, but he was just as much a part of this as his best friend. Mark and Rich knew the same stories and legends about what was in the forest on the far east side of town. He wanted to test their validity just as much as Rich did.

There weren't supposed to be creatures like what the two had conjured from the woods. The whole ritual thing was intended to be a joke. Mark was interested in the folklore but never thought they'd really pull it off. He didn't know it was possible.

They were a couple of kids looking to kill time on a warm summer evening, having fun with a local legend. The boys heard the story countless times in their short twelve years from parents, uncles, older kids, and even the local clergy. The story of the Wendigo.

Mark remembered Father Anthony telling the legend in Sunday school as an example of how god protected those who served him, a classic clergy scare tactic that, like most things, he told the children, wasn't true. No amount of faith could keep the Wendigo away.

It was rumored the malevolent creature began roaming the nearby forest after settlers pushed the Native Americans off their own land, edging them further out until they were secluded on the far east side of what became the eventual town. The Natives resided there without incident until the following season when the town folk decided to get rid of them for good.

The natives were caught off guard by the sneak attack, forced to surrender, and driven from the land entirely, but as they left, the shaman warned the townspeople of a creature called the Wendigo who roamed the forest surrounding them.

Without the tribe to perform seasonal rituals to keep the beast at bay, the Wendigo would pass the curse of its hunger to the townfolk, turning them all into flesh-eating maniacs as punishment. When the shaman turned to leave, the town's ragtag militia unloaded their muskets into his back. He fell face first on the path, where the dirt and blood mixed into red runny sludge. A ghastly howl erupted from somewhere deep in the woods, and some straggling tribesman quickly snatched up the shaman's body, disappearing with it into the forest.

Then, all hell broke loose.

That night, under darkness, the Wendigo slunk into town and possessed a sleeping woman with a fraction of the powerful hunger he was eternally cursed with. By morning, she'd killed and eaten her two children and was working on eating her husband when discovered by a neighbor. They attempted to pull her away from the partially devoured corpse, but she snapped and snarled at anyone who got close.

Eight of the strongest men in town came in to try and overtake her, but she dashed past them and flung herself through the window before they could make a move. They rushed outside and found the woman lying dead in a crumpled heap below the window with a broken neck and shards of glass sunk deep through her face.

Some believed the devil had taken over the woman, while others rationalized her behavior due to a severe mental disorder, but the Wendigo would prove them all wrong. Two nights later, the beast slogged into town to curse another community member with a piece of his insatiable hunger, and this time was seen. It was brief, but the eyewitness account was enough to scare the town into taking the shaman's warning seriously.

Thomas had been sleeping soundly when a sudden chill snapped him awake. A troubled stirring in his gut got him out of bed to drink water from the pitcher next to the window.

He gulped greedily, absently pushed the curtains aside, and saw it. The creature walked upright on two legs, taller than any man he'd ever seen, and while gaunt and sickly, didn't appear to be suffering.

Coarse, black, matted hair covered the ultra-thin body save for where ribs visibly poked through the thin skin stretched across them. The Wendigo's head resembled a man with a massive entanglement of antlers springing from its top like a deer, only far more vicious. The horns twisted into points at the ends and dripped blood that looked black in the moonlight.

Eyes dark and shiny like onyx orbs were set deep into its oddly proportioned face, and a quick snarl showed a snout filled with pointy spikes too long and sharp to be teeth, yet they jutted from the thing's mouth. Thomas watched the creature skulk in long, loping strides that landed hard against the earth but made no sound. The Wendigo walked up to the Proctor's house, tore the door from its hinges without hesitation, and crashed through the opening.

Overcome by fear, Thomas fainted and awoke on the floor in front of the window in the morning. He'd remembered what he saw and rushed outside to find a small crowd gathered around the destroyed doorway of the Proctor house. Thomas started up the path and opened his mouth to call out but was cut off by a scream followed by a shot. Both came from inside the home.

Some people stepped away from the door, covering their mouths and crying, while others averted their eyes, looking anywhere but inside the house. The Wendigo had put a piece of its hunger into the youngest Proctor boy, Timothy, who was six years old. Sometimes, Timothy subdued his mother, father, and two sisters, consuming much of their flesh.

The boy hadn't eaten any of his family members entirely but instead took bites from different parts of them as if trying to decide which tasted better. A neighbor woman drawing water from the well noticed the door was gone from the house and walked up to check on the family. Aghast by the scene, she ran to get help while the boy barricaded himself in the back room with his meal.

The shot Thomas heard put the boy down after he lunged at the men trying to get to him, slashing one of them deeply across the forearm with only his fingernails. Thomas told them what he'd seen the night before, and suddenly, the notion of the Wendigo's curse was taken seriously.

After the Proctor Family incident, several families packed what they could carry and searched for another settlement to join. Those who stayed put together a party of the strongest, highly skilled hunters left in the town and set out the following night to conquer the beast that plagued their community.

The following day, a sole member of the hunting party was found in the field at the forest's edge. The other men's bodies littered around him while he eats the detached arm. The mangled corpses were missing large portions of skin, with a significant amount of the muscle beneath being ripped away.

He was naked and covered in blood to the extent he more resembled a demon escaped from Hell than a man. He snarled, gnashing his teeth at those who'd come to see what turned out to be another blood bath.

They didn't speak or try to reason with the surviving hunter and shot him in the head on sight. They left the bodies in the field and hurried home to gather what they could for a hasty exit. A man named James Smyth halted the mass exodus, claiming he knew a way to rid the town of the Wendigo for good but warned to do so, he would have to consort with dark forces. Smyth studied ancient sigil magic for years but kept it a carefully guarded secret to avoid persecution.

The remaining townsfolk were skeptical, fearing the man would only bring greater evil down upon them, but decided to let Smyth make his attempt by nightfall. He gathered the items he would need in a leather sack, took one of the two goats he owned, and went out in the forest alone to banish the Wendigo.

The next day, the townspeople waited at the wood's edge as the sun rose for Smyth to return, hoping for good news. It wasn't long before he stumbled out of the forest naked, covered with symbols drawn in blood, while proclaiming his success. The goat was absent, but the Wendigo was no more.

The townspeople believed him but remained skittish and unsure until an entire week passed without another incident. Smyth was graciously thanked, and an understanding was established wherein they would look the other way when it came to him practicing magic if he kept it strictly within the four walls of his home.

Life continued, and the town saw the eventual return of many who'd left once news of the vanquished Wendigo spread. James Smyth spent most of his time alone in his home, secluded on the far west edge of town. Slowly, he began to lose his mind over the coming months, claiming to be tormented by angry spirits he'd unintentionally provoked.

His health deteriorated, and before the year was out, James Smyth was dead. On his deathbed, he confessed to the town's priest that he'd lied about banishing the Wendigo and had only trapped it using a magic circle. He'd tried to send it away, but none of his spells worked, so he left it within the circle, trapped between planes until someone or something let it out again.

The priest brought this information to the small council formed after the Wendigo incident, hoping they'd be prepared if the creature ever returned. The confession remained a secret for some time, but as these things go, the information was leaked, perhaps with the encouragement of a strong drink, and before long, the entire town was aware of Smyth's untruth.

Hence, the legend was passed down throughout the years in a generational game of telephone. There wasn't a kid in town who hadn't heard multiple versions of the Wendigo story, but taking them seriously was tantamount to believing in Santa Claus. It was a story to scare their little brothers or sisters just as it had been done to them.

Mark neared the front pew, wishing he'd believed as a kid because even a small amount of fear might have been enough to keep Rich and him from trying anything involving the Wendigo. The bowl was on the altar beyond the pulpit, putting Mark mere feet away from the prize. The only issue was Father Anthony.

The priest was five feet beyond the altar on his knees with his back to Mark, and the chunky slop of what had been an altar boy named Bryan was on the floor in front of him. He tore chunks of flesh and muscle with his hands, greedily stuffing them into his face. Mark held his breath, hoping not to be heard over the slurping sounds of a boy being unceremoniously devoured in a place that existed solely based on ceremony.

If he could get the bowl without alerting Father Anthony of his presence, he'd be able to carefully sneak back out of the church. Otherwise, he was prepared to grab it and run for his life. The priest leaned forward, his head down into the open torso of the boy like a pig eating from a trough. When he pulled his head back up, Mark saw a kidney dangling by its connective tissue from between Father Anthony's teeth before the hunger-possessed priest sucked the organ up to his mouth.

He chomped down, and the kidney burst, spraying translucent red fluid from his open maw. He swallowed and plunged his head back into the hollow cavity to suss out the kidney's mate, gulping up blood and viscera. Mark knew he wouldn't get a better chance than this and lunged into action, capitalizing on the moment.

He leapt up the four steps to the altar two at a time and slowly crept to the bowl. Mark was close enough to reach out and grab the final object needed to end the terror he and his best friend unleashed upon the town.

He held his breath and carefully brought his hand forward, trying to ignore the sickening sounds of mastication from a few feet before him. Father Anthony's face was still deep in the mess he'd made of the boy's insides lapping up remnants of the inflicted carnage, but he snapped up the instant Mark's hand contacted the bowl.

The priest flung his head around, sending a tremendous spray of blood across the altar, spattering the shiny silver bowl with tiny crimson dots that spread into shapeless blobs against the mirrored surface. A few drops hit Mark in the face, and the coppery bite of blood burned his lips as he inadvertently ran his tongue across them.

His faltering hesitation allowed Father Anthony to leap to his feet and address the fresh news before him. Mark grabbed the bowl, jumped down the steps, and hit the ground running with the priest right behind. He didn't need to look back to see how close Father Anthony was because he felt the wretched hot breath on the back of his neck. He was already on Mark's heels.

Father Anthony bellowed a throaty gravel-laced howl as he ran up the aisle, staying just a step behind the boy. Mark crashed against the heavy wooden door, only it didn't open as fast as he'd hoped, halting his momentum. Father Anthony collided with him, having also not anticipated the sudden stop, but the added weight behind the impact helped push the door open and throw Mark through.

The priest's face took the brunt, which sent him falling backward while Mark stumbled over the threshold and tumbled down the six concrete steps that led up to the church. He tucked the bowl close to his chest as he fell, refusing to let go until he could put it in Rich's hand. He popped up immediately upon hitting the sidewalk, adrenaline blotting out the pain. He didn't have time to be hurt.

Father Anthony launched through the open door a moment later and landed on the sidewalk, skipping the steps completely. The daylight exposed angles of the priest's horridly grotesque features kept hidden by the dimness of the sanctuary. His face was a dripping red wash of the altar boy's blood, and his eyes popped wide and wild against the contrast. He snarled, baring teeth smeared with gore red as his face while a segment of partially eaten small intestine dangled from the side of his mouth like an upside-down snorkel.

His white collar had gone red from the blood running down his face and chin slicking, his cassock with the stuff from his shoulders to his feet. The thin, wet material clung tight to his arms and chest, showing musculature that usually hid beneath billowing robes swallowed by folds of fabric. Mark didn't realize how strong Father Anthony was; clearly, the man spent time in the gym.

Mark allowed himself only a quick glance before sprinting in the opposite direction. He felt being out in the open would help him elude the priest, but he'd need to be on the lookout. Others were running around with the Wendigo's hunger within them. When he reached the end of the block, the pounding of Father Anthony's footfalls didn't sound as close anymore, but he didn't dare slow up. When he turned right at the corner, Mark heard a scream and couldn't keep from turning to look.

Father Anthony stood in a front yard four houses back, using his teeth to rip the throat of an old woman who'd been weeding her garden when the two ran by. He must have sensed she'd be an easier meal to catch and pounced.

Mark saw a red mist fill the air around the two as Father Anthony yanked his head back, ripping flesh and opening veins. He must have gotten a portion of the windpipe in his first bite because her screaming stopped as suddenly as it started.

The last thing Mark saw before continuing down the intersecting street was an old man, presumably the woman's husband, who came out the front door onto the porch waving his arms, shuffling as fast as he could across the yard toward the crimson-sprayed carnage. The priest dropped the woman to the ground, and the old man stopped in his tracks. Before he could turn to shuffle away, Father Anthony was already sinking his teeth into the soft waddle of flesh dangling from the man's chin.

Mark rounded the corner before seeing blood spray from the man's severed jugular, but he had no trouble picturing it. The next block appeared empty as Mark raced past the row of houses, but it was different when he made a left on Spruce Street toward the forest.

Windows were broken, and doors lay in yards where they'd landed after being ripped from their hinges to extract the meaty morsels that were the people living inside. Mark glanced to his left and saw the bloody pulp of what had been Mr. Williams lying across the concrete path leading from the sidewalk to his front door.

The red and pink mush was unrecognizable as random flesh, tissue, and remnants of organs were mashed together to form the outline of a person. Mark knew it was Mr. Williams because a portion of his waist-length, dirty-blonde hair extended from the top of his faceless skull like the plume of a fallen knight's helmet.

He heard growls and the crashing of furniture coming from inside the doorless Williams' house and picked up his pace despite the burning muscles in his legs, screaming to relent his taxing assault on them. He could see the break in the tree line at the dead-end that would lead him to Rich and the end of this nightmare.

He dashed past the last house on the left, and an unsavory version of Judith Carmichael was crouched over another bloodied victim face down on their stomach. She was tearing a long strip of flesh from their back with her teeth when Mark raced by, and while she howled and gnashed her bloody teeth at him, she remained with her kill.

He jumped through the opening in the trees, elated the woman had chosen not to pursue him, and booked it up the trail to deliver the last item needed to put the Wendigo to rest. Mark followed the curve in the path and saw Rich thirty yards ahead, waiting for him in the small clearing just as they'd planned.

His back was to Mark as he faced the altar, no doubt busying himself with final touches while waiting for the bowl. Mark tried to call out but couldn't make any sound between gasps and opted to reach his destination before speaking. He slowed upon reaching the clearing and clomped to a hard stop in the final feet of his approach.

"I . . ." Mark attempted while panting. "I . . . got . . . it."

He bent over to catch his breath and held the bowl out with one hand while the other rested on his knee. Rich didn't acknowledge and continued tweaking the altar, his back still turned.

"Hey!" Mark managed with more strength behind his voice. "I said—"

Mark suddenly realized his friend wasn't doing anything with the altar, which lay toppled in pieces just beyond Rich's standing. He heard the sound next, the same sickeningly wet chewing he'd heard back at the church. He clutched the bowl to his chest and stepped back as Rich turned around. He held an arm with grizzled stretched flaps of skin dangling like bicycle streamers at the shoulder from being pulled until snapping free.

Rich had his left hand around the forearm while his right gripped below the bicep with his face down in the ditch of its elbow in a morbid mockery of eating a giant slice of watermelon. He pulled back, tearing tendon and muscle from bone, froze when he saw Mark, and let the long strings of meat dangle from his teeth before slurping them into his mouth.

The boy's eyes were rimmed in red and no longer his own. The Wendigo had him. Rich wailed, ejecting flecks of blood-speckled gristle from a mouth that opened too wide to be human anymore.

Mark dropped the bowl, turned down the path, and started running. ☠

HAPPY BIRTHDAY

The front room was dark, but he no longer left lights on in the house. Curtis engaged the deadbolt after closing the door and stood still in the darkness, holding his breath and listening.

Satisfied by several seconds of uninterrupted silence, Curtis slipped off his dark gray wool blazer, the only one he wore when he left the house, and tossed it over a stack of boxes in the entryway. The room used to be a place he liked to sit down with a cold beer and listen to his records. Sometimes, he'd have a friend or two over to join him for a good ol' bull session, but Curtis had long since stopped caring about these things.

The room was cluttered with boxes while random pieces of furniture stacked with laundry baskets of dirty clothes filled the spaces between. The area was no longer suited for gatherings or conversation, which was fine by Curtis since he didn't have any more friends or interest in making new ones. He'd come to loathe entertaining almost as much as the people he'd entertained.

He navigated a narrow path through the clutter and stepped into the living room but stopped when he heard something. He strained his ears, hoping the sound had been imagined, but he wasn't taking any chances. After a full minute of silence, he decided it must have come from the shifting mess and left it at that.

He passed a switch on his way to the kitchen but didn't turn on the lights. Curtis was comfortable in the dark, and light would only let his neighbors know he was home. He hated people knowing his business. Less interaction with people meant less of a chance something could go wrong, and Curtis was too close to risk losing it all because some local idiot stopped by to borrow a cup of sugar.

The shine on the linoleum kitchen floor had been dulled by months of unchecked grime, and moonlight streaming through the window above the sink revealed a fuzzy texture growing atop the layer of filth. He stepped to the counter and retrieved a dirty plastic cup. He filled it with water from the sink, drank it all, then repeated the action. When he set the cup back on the counter, something on the outside left his fingers sticky, and he wiped them up and down the side of his slacks.

Curtis turned around, leaned against the sink with his arms crossed, and faced the door to the basement. He couldn't help but smile, a subconscious reflex whenever the basement happened to cross his mind. It wasn't the basement itself, but what was in it, or who, rather, that brought about his insuppressible joy.

The sound came again, and this time was decidedly not imagined. The ends of Curtis's smile pulled downward while the rest of the muscles in his face resituated to form a complementary expression. The sound wasn't loud, barely audible, but as far as Curtis was concerned, it was deafening. It sounded like shuffling cardboard with the tiniest hint of squeaking, like you'd hear from a rusty hinge.

The noise was so subtle only Curtis would've been able to hear it, but he also knew what he was listening for. His breaths turned shallow, but he pushed the air out hard through his nose before parting his lips to even the flow.

He stomped to the basement door, threw it open, and stared down the steps into the darkness. It was louder now, and someone was in the basement crying. The noise quickly cut off, and Curtis's breathing became heavier and louder.

"What did I say about bein' quiet, huh? What did I say about cryin'?" He screamed from the top of the stairs.

He pawed at a switch on the wall to his right, and a single bulb at the base of the stairs lit up, casting a dull yellow glow on the concrete floor. One of the floor drains Curtis installed was there, and the low light reflected off the tangled clumps of long black hair clogging its holes.

Before descending the stairs, he grabbed his homemade blade from where it hung next to the light switch. He'd made the weapon by duct-taping a wooden handle to two feet of a tree saw blade from which he'd broken the original handle. The spaces between the differently angled teeth of the blade were caked with partially dry skin and damp tissue, and Curtis banged it against the wall to shake the clinging chunks loose.

The squeal came again in Pavlovian response to the sound of the blade smacking the wall.

"You're only making it worse," he called out.

Curtis was halfway down the stairs before he could smell it, but the stench wasn't as foul since he'd installed the drains and taken to hosing the basement down every other night. The smell was a potpourri of co-mingled shit, piss, sweat, and blood with a healthy dose of death to bind it all together. It was already stuffy down there, but something had to be done when the smell got to where he could not stand it.

The drains were a bitch and a half to put in by himself and took two whole weeks, but they worked like a charm. He used pine-scented cleanser the first couple of times he cleaned, but the mixed aromas made him sick, so he switched to plain, unscented dish soap. It did the trick and kept the smell from making its way up into the house.

Curtis flipped another switch at the bottom of the steps, and a second bare bulb sizzled to life in the center of the ceiling, casting a similarly dull light across most of the basement. The blade fell from his hand and clattered against the concrete floor when he saw empty chains hanging from the ceiling. When he left for work that morning, a woman was dangling from the chains by her wrists. He was sure of it.

Eight hours ago, she was in and out of consciousness, barely alive with no idea where she was, but now she was gone. Curtis's eyes scanned back and forth and saw no sign of the woman, but she couldn't hide in many places. Thinking she'd fled, he turned and lunged for the stairs but stopped short.

He'd heard something coming from the basement in the kitchen and again even louder while standing at the top of the steps. And he heard it again right now. Someone was down there with him or something.

"Is that you, darlin'?" He stepped away from the stairs and back toward the open space in the middle of the cellar. "I can hear you, so I know it is."

Curtis cautiously approached the hanging chains, studying the shadows for movement, when he realized something didn't make sense. If the woman was free, which she obviously was, why would she stay in the basement?

He thought there might be a slim possibility he'd arrived home just at the right moment to spoil her getaway, but that was too easy. He knew better than to think things would work out in his favor. Nothing worked out in Curtis's favor, but his luck was about to change, or at least it would if the woman didn't get away.

He contemplated what might be her motivation to stay. There was a chance she'd had been too weak to make it up the stairs, having expended the last of her energy escaping the chains.

Maybe she'd crawled into a corner to crouch in the deepest part of the shadows, hoping he'd run back upstairs so she could slip away while he searched for her? Curtis fingered one of the chains and turned slowly on his heel, peering into the darkness behind him.

What worried him most was the woman stuck around, not because she was too exhausted to move, but because she wanted revenge. She could've been free for hours and spent the day crafting the perfect plan to exact vengeance upon him.

Curtis suddenly felt extra vulnerable and backed toward the stairs until he reached where he'd dropped his blade. He grabbed the weapon and brandished it before him, holding it ready.

"You may as well come out on out now," Curtis said, swiping at the air with the busted tree-blade, each swing accompanied by a metallic rush of air. "You're gonna' have a much tougher time if I pull you out from where you're hidin'. Best just give up now, or I'll make you wish you were dead."

There was a single beat of silence before the noise came again from a pile of dirty rags bunched together in the far-left corner. It was the same shuffling sound with a squeal, but even up close, he couldn't discern the cause.

The pile was not large enough for a person to hide under. Not even a child could fully conceal themself, but Curtis couldn't take any chances. He stalked toward the corner, his blade held high, his eyes on the rags. He was within three feet when he thought he perceived a shift in the pile and began whacking wildly with his sawblade. The rags flew to the side, and two became snagged in his weapon's sharp-angled teeth. Just as he'd suspected, no one was there, and he tore the rags from the blade, tossing the shreds over his shoulder.

Curtis stepped to the corner for a closer look, expecting to find what was left of some pest or vermin, but what he saw turned his body numb. There was a single word crudely scratched into the concrete floor in thin, jagged strokes that said: UPSTAIRS

Curtis was momentarily paralyzed from shock, and the skin of his extremities tightened into dimpled gooseflesh.

His wits returned a beat later, and he spun around, expecting to find someone behind him, but there was no one. He looked over his shoulder at the writing on the floor and heard the sound again, but now it came from the top of the stairs. His stomach twisted, sending a gurgle from his bowels, and Curtis realized he was scared.

He had no control over whatever was happening, whatever this was, which was a difficult and uncomfortable feeling to process. Curtis flashed to other situations in his life where he'd had no control. His failed marriage, dead-end job, and utterly useless and unfulfilling place in life were all outside his controlling grasp. He viewed himself as a failure as little by little, these pieces of him were wrenched away and flushed down the toilet by the Universe.

That was in the past. Curtis had taken back the control he'd lost or given away, and he'd be goddamned if he was going to lose it again.

"I don't like games," he called out, even-toned. "I never have. You wanna know why? Because I think they're a waste of time. I don't like wastin' my time."

His fear morphed into anger, and he stepped lightly to the stairs to avoid making noise. He stopped short of the banister and listened, but the basement was quiet as a tomb, and when he crouched to peek up the stairs from around the railing, no one was there.

Not only that, the door at the top of the stairs was closed. He hadn't closed the door behind him, and now there was no doubt the woman was still in the house. She was upstairs and had probably been up there the whole time. His face went hot as his anger flared to full-blown rage. He was ending this now. He was in control.

Curtis flew up the stairs two at a time and barreled into the door with his shoulder without breaking momentum. It exploded open as the latch ripped the strike plate from the frame. As he expected, the kitchen was completely dark, but as soon as his feet touched the linoleum, the room burst into bright light.

"Surprise!"

The cadre of voices surrounded him on all sides, and he furiously blinked against the sudden brightness, forcing his irises to rapidly make the necessary adjustments.

When his vision cleared, he continued to blink, unwilling and unable to believe what he saw. The woman from the basement, the one he'd been after, stood four feet before him and held a cake. Curtis recognized the swollen purple lump he'd turned her face into and saw her eyes looking through slits between the distended tissue surrounding them. There were long, jagged lacerations down her exposed thighs from whipping her with a chain length. Curtis liked to keep the wounds open and fresh without allowing time for them to heal.

The woman held up the cake, displaying it for him to see. Her small breasts were covered in crisscrossing scratches, and one of her nipples looked like a wad of chewed black bubblegum. Curtis looked down at the cake where the words *Happy Birthday* were written in pink frosting flanked between two twinkling yellow candles.

But it wasn't just the woman waiting for him in the kitchen; it was all of them. Every one of the people he'd taken to his basement over the last three years was crowded around, filling nearly every inch of space. Their attempted smiles through mangled mouths achieved uniquely unsettling expressions, intensifying the already horrific sight of their faces.

Despite having distorted their features through a multitude of savage methods, Curtis recognized and remembered each one of

them. He didn't know their names, but that was because of his own rule. He didn't want to know names and took the necessary measures to ensure he never found out.

Wallets, purses, backpacks, Curtis burned these things in the barrel in his backyard without ever going through them. He knew he was destroying cash, among other valuable items, but this wasn't about money. Curtis wanted nothing from the people he brought to his basement but their life. He didn't need their money, and he didn't need to know their names.

He could distinguish the victims in his kitchen in other ways, like the man to his left with no arms, a melted face, and wearing a pink and purple party hat. His face was like that because Curtis threw a pot of boiling cooking oil into it, and he had no arms because he'd been left hanging from the chains after he died until they fell off. The party hat was a new contradicting addition.

A torso covered in sagging gray flesh leaned against the legs of the woman holding the cake. Skin hung from the stumps in putrid, jagged strips on account of the method used to remove the limbs. Curtis had found the dullest chainsaw blade he could and dulled it even more before making the amputations. The man was still alive when he started.

He remembered, even with the chain running at full power, having to saw back and forth through the muscle and bone to fully sever muscle and bone. Curtis recalled the man's tormented shrieks rising to an ear-piercing crescendo before he finally bled out enough to die. Then, Curtis cut his head off.

He'd removed flesh from the bones of the arms and legs, ground it up with his own personal meat grinder, and made two hundred burger patties from all the meat. A day later, Curtis donated the meat and his time to the Catholic Church two streets over, where he personally cooked and served each burger during their annual 'Back to School Youth Picnic'.

He'd never received so many compliments on his cooking and was asked by several parishioners if he was interested in catering their upcoming events. While he might have entertained the thought for a moment, he ultimately declined. He'd achieved what he set out to do that day, and while feeding man-meat to an unsuspecting group of do-gooders was satisfying, it was a hell of a lot of work. He hadn't used the man's head in his culinary experiment and vaguely wondered what had happened to it until he looked up and saw it on the counter.

The head was leaned against the coffee maker at a precarious angle balanced between it and the backsplash. A lipless mouth formed a lopsided 'O', revealing jagged, useless stumps of yellow and brown teeth. Curtis remembered wearing steel-toed boots when he'd kicked them all those months ago.

A paper party hat, gold with red stripes, sat perched atop the head sideways, nearly falling off. A green nub was all that remained of the man's tongue, and it bobbed up and down in the toothless hole, struggling to free itself from the cavern of rot.

Curtis detected smoke and looked to the right, where one of his more recent victims was standing. The woman's abdomen was a charred gaping hole that opened into blackened, unrecognizable insides. Dark gray smoke meandered hypnotically from the opening in thin, wavy wisps.

He'd sliced the woman across the stomach first, then used his hands to pull the flesh apart, widening the wound. She was still alive, but not much longer after Curtis jammed a lit road flare inside the hole he'd created. A flare can burn for up to sixty minutes, even in inclement weather conditions, and he watched rapturously as this one burned for forty-three minutes and thirteen seconds.

Large weeping blisters pushed out from the skin on her chest and shoulders like bulbous misshapen tumors while the flare's flame burned her from the inside out. Her eyes were bulging smoky marbles, leaking thick yellow tears while the skin on her face flaked away like burnt paper. She looked remarkably the same standing in front of him now as she did then, only that shouldn't be possible. None of this should.

Curtis looked across the mangled faces of the people he'd killed while his mind reeled and his pulse quickened. It was impossible for them to be alive. They couldn't have risen from shallow hidden graves because there were no graves to rise from.

Curtis didn't bury the bodies of his victims. Instead, he put them in fifty-gallon steel drums with a mixture of Nitric and Oxalic acids and lye to turn the remains into a watery slurry easily poured down the largest of the drains he'd installed. All the people standing in his kitchen looked as they had before going into the barrel, and Curtis strained to grasp what was happening.

In unison, they all began to groan and grunt, and it took several seconds for Curtis to realize they were singing Happy Birthday. The words were pronounced as best they could through the various unpleasant sounds made by dead and destroyed vocal cords. The generally happy song became a haunted, unsettling dirge that soured his stomach.

"What is this?" Curtis cried out to the singing horde. "What do you want? Why are you doing this?"

The woman held the cake out to Curtis again, the candles now runny puddles of wax, and took a shambling step forward while continuing to sing. The rest of the group followed suit, advancing toward the birthday boy as a single unit. Curtis stepped back, forgetting how close he was to the top of the basement steps, until he started tumbling down them.

He fell head over heels and caught small glimpses of his victims crowded around the door, still singing, the woman with the cake front and center leading the pack.

His head smacked against the concrete floor at the base of the stairs on an angle, and his neck snapped, killing him instantly before he could see the doorframe at the top of the steps was empty. The woman was still hung by chains from the ceiling.

She screamed when she saw Curtis hit the floor and screamed even harder when she realized he was dead. She screamed until no life was left in her, and the house was quiet again, just like Curtis liked it. ☠

NEW FRIENDS

enny had no idea why the twins suddenly wanted to play with him, and apprehension overshadowed any excitement he might've felt at the opportunity. He was nine while the twins, Pauline and Jessica, were twelve, and the girls typically ignored Benny, shunning his attempts at friendship. He'd stopped trying to interact with them months ago and avoided them whenever possible.

He would stay in if he saw them outside from his window and even went to the lengths of crossing the street or taking the long way home to avoid being taunted and threatened by the sisters. He did his best to ignore the girls, but they didn't make it easy. Lately, though, Benny hadn't seen the twins around the neighborhood and was unsure if he should be happy or nervous. They only lived three houses down from his, which was a little too close for comfort as far as he was concerned.

The only other kid on the block close to Benny's age was Marcus, who was ten. The boys were in the same grade despite the age difference since Marcus had been held back a year, and the two's friendship was mostly a byproduct of proximity. Still, they got along well enough and enjoyed each other's company. Benny had just started to relax and let his guard down when the twins showed up at his door Saturday morning.

He was expecting Marcus when his mother called up the stairs to tell him he had company, which was why it was so jarring when he saw Pauline and Jessica's identical smiling faces on the porch instead.

"Benny dear," his mom said, also smiling. "The girls came over to see if you wanted to come out to play with them. Isn't that nice? I told them you would be delighted."

Benny was aghast at what he was hearing. The twins *wanted* to play with him? The contradiction was shocking, and he searched their faces for signs of veiled contempt.

"I . . . I, uh . . ." Benny looked from the girls to his mom struggling to put a response together. "I was su—"

"Oh, don't tell me you were supposed to play with Marcus today," his mother's smile dropped as she moved her hands to her hips. "You play with him all the time, plus I don't think he's a good influence on you."

"Marcus got held back in school, you know," Pauline said through a saccharine smile.

"Our mom said it's because he has behavior issues," added Jessica on the heels of her sister's unnecessary statement.

"I know girls, I know," Benny's mother replied, nodding, her smile returned.

The truth was Marcus had been held back not for his behavior but because the school he'd attended the year before moving to the neighborhood used a different curriculum. He wasn't adequately prepared for the standardized tests his new school required and failed them miserably. They decided holding Marcus back was what he needed to get caught up to the rest of his classmates.

"Here, honey," Benny's mother said, taking his red jacket from the hook on the wall and handing it to him. "It's chilly out there today."

The twins wore hooded sweatshirts matching in design but differing in color, with Pauline in black and Jessica in orange. His mother helped him into his jacket, pushing him out the door and onto the porch with the twins. His eyes darted back and forth between the two of them, unsure what to make of the strange situation.

"Sooooooo," Benny let the word drag out while thinking about what to say next. "What did you two want to play? I have a tetherball pole set up in the backyard."

The girls exchanged a look, their smiles unwavering.

"We had a different kind of game in mind," said Jessica.

"Different and really fun," Pauline added.

"Different?" Benny buried his hands in the pockets of his jacket. "What do you mean by 'different'?"

"It's kind of hard to explain," Pauline said.

"It's better if we show you," Jessica continued.

"Show me? Well, okay."

Benny's initial reticence began to wane as his curiosity took over, and he wondered if perhaps this was the beginning of an actual friendship? Maybe they were done torturing him and wanted to turn over a new leaf?

"Follow us!" The girls sang in unison as they skipped from the porch across the lawn.

"Where are we going?" Benny jogged to catch up.

"We're going to our house," Jessica called over her shoulder.

"The game is set up in our basement," Pauline added. "It's so fun. We can't wait to show you."

Benny chased the twins around the side of their house into the backyard, where they stopped at the basement door. It was slanted at an angle nearly horizontal to the ground, and Jessica bent to pull the door by its handle while her sister held it open, motioning Benny down the dark stairs. He hesitated until Jessica stepped inside. Her head momentarily disappeared beneath the ground, then popped back into the sunlight.

"Come on," she said. "This is gonna' be so fun!"

"Okay, I'm coming."

Benny felt a surge of anticipatory excitement as he approached the open door, and his earlier reservations melted into the background of a potentially new relationship. He started down the steps behind Jessica, and Pauline followed, letting the door slam shut. An impossibly inky black darkness clamped around Benny with a stale and stifling thickness, but his fear was muted by frenzied exhilaration.

He paused, unsure what to do next, when a candle flared to life and floated toward him with Jessica's fingers wrapped around the base. Another small flame appeared beside it as Pauline lit a second candle and stood beside her sister. The candles were short and thin, but not as thin as birthday cake candles, which were black. Benny had never seen black candles before.

"Are you ready?" Jessica asked.

The twins' faces assumed a dark countenance, the tiny flames highlighting a malevolence in their expressions. Doubt tried to creep back into Benny's mind at the frightful sight, but he denied it, refusing to let himself freak out for no reason.

"What's that smell?" He asked, forcing his mind to focus on anything else.

He'd caught a whiff of something when he reached the bottom of the stairs, and the scent was quite pungent with the door closed. It reminded him of rotten trash mixed with sweet musk, which had most likely been used to try and cover it up.

"There was a pipe leaking down here for a while before our dad noticed," Jessica chimed as Pauline moved to the center of the room.

"And he found a dead rat too," Pauline said, touching the flame of her candle to others arranged in a circle on the floor, igniting their wicks one by one. "The carcass was under the leak, so the rat rotted *and* liquified. It looked so cool!"

"Yeah, it did," her sister continued. "Dad was supposed to have it professionally cleaned but hasn't gotten around to it, so we've been using incense to cover the smell."

"Which works out perfectly," Pauline said, lighting the final candle on the floor, "because burning incense is part of the game."

The candles added some light, but the room truly brightened when Pauline lit a larger candle attached to the far wall of the basement. Benny's eyes readjusted to the candle's diffused light and saw three masks hanging above.

The features were wrapped in angled shadows, obscuring the details and making them appear monstrous. The pungent scent of incense grew stronger, and Benny saw Pauline lighting more of it in the center of the circle of candles. He stepped toward the twins and paused to see what was drawn within the circle. The nagging dread returned, tugging at the base of his stomach. He'd seen plenty of horror movies with pentagrams and understood what he was looking at. He just didn't know why?

"Is this part of the game?" Benny tried to sound aloof and sarcastic at the same time. "Are we casting spells or something?"

"No fair," Jessica whined. "You figured it out."

"That's okay," Pauline said, turning to the candle on the wall. "He didn't ruin the surprise."

She stood on tiptoes and reached up to remove the masks one by one.

"You're right, you're right," Jessica giggled. "There's still the surprise!"

"What's the surprise?" Benny's voice wavered, his nerves betraying him.

"If we told you, it wouldn't be a surprise." Pauline returned with the masks and stood by her sister across the circle from Benny. "And that wouldn't be any fun at all."

Pauline gave a mask to her sister, handed one to Benny, and kept one for herself. The light was still low, but Benny could see the masks well enough to recognize them. They were made of wood with thick pieces of twine attached on each side to secure it to the wearer's face.

The mask he held was of a sheep, or at least the best approximation of one the materials used to construct it would allow. The snout was painted light pink with a black dot for a nose in the center, while the rest was white with uneven lumps of texture meant to be tufts of wool. Perfect circles no bigger than quarters had been cut for eyeholes, and two triangle-shaped bulges jutted from the top of the mask for ears.

He ran his fingers across the inside of the mask and felt the cracks in the lacquer used to seal the wood. Benny hadn't seen anything like this in stores, including the seasonal Halloween mega-store that opened next to the pharmacy every year. There were hundreds, even thousands of masks, but none like what he held now. This was delicate yet solid. At first glance, it appeared to be pieced together, but he could find no seams along the inside.

The rotten rat smell returned, and Benny put his hand over his mouth and nose.

"Oh man," he choked. "Are you sure your dad got that rat out of he—"

Benny flinched when he looked up, not expecting the twins to be wearing identical wolf masks. The sharp-angled features he'd glimpsed when they hung from the wall gave them an incredibly terrifying quality in the flickering candlelight.

The mouths were made into fixed snarls showing off many pointed teeth within. Their texture was like the simulated wool on the sheep mask. Only the edges were straight and stiff, while his were soft and rounded. Reflected yellow candlelight danced in the twins' eyes as they glared through the holes of their masks.

"If you put your mask on, it helps with the smell."

Benny couldn't tell which mask the sound was coming out of and wasn't sure which girl to look at or address.

"Oh, okay." He brought the mask to his face and hesitated. "Is this part of the game?"

"Yes," said one twin.

"It's the best part of the game," said her sister.

Benny looked from the eyes of one wolf to the other and took a deep breath. He brought the mask to his face and tightened the twine against the back of his head. The underside was cold and slick, and he hoped the cracks in the finish wouldn't leave tiny cuts on his face. The eyeholes offered nothing in the way of peripheral vision further, obstructing what little he could see in the dim light.

They were right about the mask helping with the smell, and the inside had its pleasant odor. The aroma was sweet and powdery but not overpoweringly so and helped ease the mild claustrophobia he felt with the awkward wooden thing hugged up around his face. The twins remained silent, their masks looking especially sinister when he saw them through the eyeholes of his own.

"Has the game started yet?" Benny looked from wolf to wolf, hoping one could provide the information. "Is there something I should be doing, or will you explain it first?"

Instead of answering, one of the masked twins bent down and picked up an old hardback book at her feet. He hadn't noticed until just then but turned her back before he could get a better look.

"We're going to start very soon." Benny recognized the voice as Pauline. "There's not much to explain, really, but you'll figure it out as we go along,"

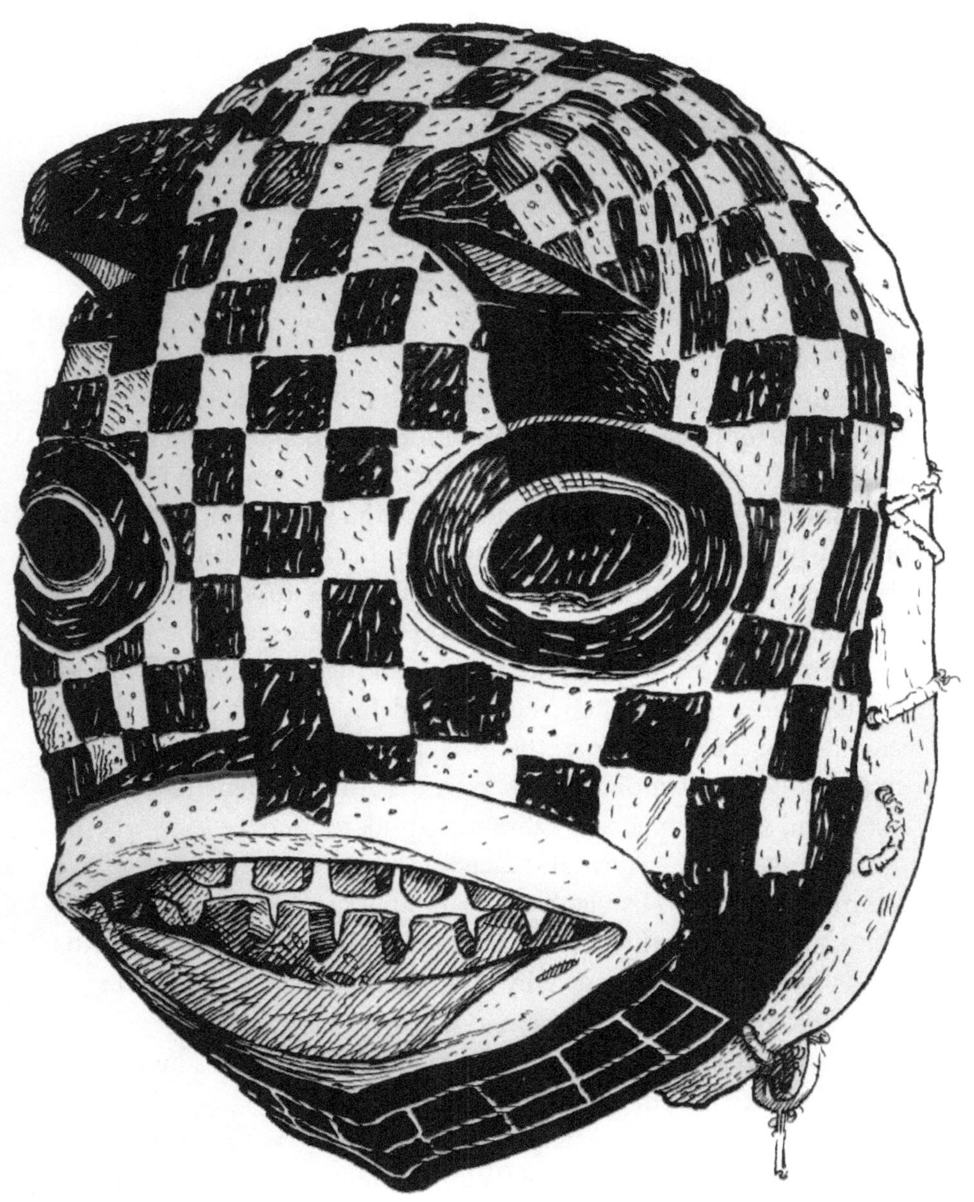

Jessica's back was still turned, her head angled down at the open book in her hands, speaking too softly for him to make out what she was saying.

"It's easy, though," continued Pauline. "You'll know exactly what to do when it's time to do it."

The basement abruptly turned cold, and an odd sensation gripped Benny's stomach. Any lingering excitement and the hope of starting an actual friendship were extinguished. The cramp in his midsection intensified, and he fell to his knees, folding over at the waist and clutching his stomach. His muscles spasmed then went tight like they were being pulled from his bones and yanked from his body.

Benny thought he could be having an allergic reaction. Perhaps the incense or mask contained something he didn't know he was allergic to, like when his cousin Eli spent the night and used the soap in Benny's shower. When he came out of the bathroom, he was covered in swollen red bumps and had a hard time breathing. A trip to the emergency room revealed he'd been allergic to a perfume in the soap but didn't know since he'd never used it before.

Benny lifted his head to the twins, looking for help, and noticed the difference immediately. He focused his eyes on the pain and saw the snarling mouths of the girls' masks were open wide. Clear strands of drool dripped slowly from the sides of their transformed maws and were lapped at by slithering pink tongues.

Their eyes were yellow and laced with a predatory countenance, their masks covered by patches of wiry gray fur, and the triangle ears moved independently atop their heads. Before his eyes, the twins' hands stretched into distortedly long shapes of thick, dangly fingers with curved black tips ending in a point.

"See, I told you he didn't ruin the surprise." The wolf's mouth was animated with articulation as it spoke.

The voice was demonically baritone with a grave resonance, but the cadence was unmistakably Pauline's. Benny tried to ask for help when a jolt of pain sent another wave of spasms through his muscles, wrenching him over at the waist, and now Benny knew there was something very wrong with this 'game'. He wasn't having an allergic reaction, but the twins were responsible for whatever was happening to him. He was in big trouble.

Benny chastised himself for not trusting his gut from the start, being gullible enough to think the twins suddenly wanted to be his friends. How could he have been so stupid? If only Marcus had shown up at his house before them, none of this would be happening. Intense nausea rolled through Benny's stomach, and he vomited.

His face was close enough to the floor to feel the warm spray of half-digested eggs and toast splash back up into his face. He heaved, purging the contents of his stomach until the bitter taste of bile filled his mouth. When the vomiting subsided, he opened his eyes to see the puddle of sick was thick with blood, and as he pushed himself away from the mess, he could move again.

Benny guessed his vomiting must've broken whatever hold they had over him and was reinvigorated by a rush of hope until he saw the twins walk around the circle toward him, or what used to be the twins. The candles around the pentagram lit their steady approach, and gray tufts of fur covered what he could see of their arms and hands before disappearing up the sleeves of their matching hoodies.

The girls' sneakers lie in shreds near the circle, their feet having become bestial paws with matching claws that clicked against the concrete floor with each step. They weren't wearing masks anymore, either. These were two honest-to-goodness wolves staring hungrily down their noses at Benny.

"Isn't this a fun game?" The subtle lilt in the wolf's mangled voice belonged to Jessica.

The hair on Benny's arms stood straight, pulling the skin aggressively tight, and his fingers curled inadvertently into fists he could not unclench. Across the basement, the staircase leading into the house appeared in the soft light like it was calling to him, offering a final chance to escape. Without thinking, Benny leapt up and lunged between the twin wolves before they could react.

He landed hard and went down on one knee but pulled himself up, motivated beyond the pain by freedom. The staircase felt miles away, but Benny pressed forward despite becoming increasingly unsteady. The most intense Charlie Horse he'd ever felt shot up his left calf, bending his foot back at the ankle, followed by the same sensation in his right leg, yet he willed himself to stay upright, determined to reach the stairs.

Benny was too focused on escape to notice the change each blast of pain delivered to his body. There would be no escape. His goose was as good as cooked the second he'd entered the basement. The 'game' Pauline and Jessica were playing was uproarious fun for them and the reason he hadn't seen them around lately.

No one in the neighborhood knew the twins' parents were amateur Satanists who occasionally dabbled in Black Magic. The twins didn't know this secret until, bored one afternoon, they decided to dig through their parents' closet while at work. Beneath a pile of clothes were boxes containing strange charms, statues, candles, and the book, among other odd totems.

The girls were fascinated by the discovery and pulled the boxes out daily to acquaint themselves with the curious discipline. The two became obsessed with learning everything they could about the mysteries of the strange items to which they were strongly attracted. It didn't take long for them to far surpass their parents' understanding of what was, for them, a passing fancy.

Soon, the girls began to apply their studies and practice what they'd learned. They started small with easy spells, temporary charms, and simple glamouring. After some trial and error, they became proficient and attempted dangerous feats of the dark arts, which was where the masks came in.

The twins read of the great significance masks played in certain rituals and ceremonies, but what really intrigued them was shapeshifting. There was a firmly held belief shared amongst seasoned practitioners of the dark arts wherein the wearer of a mask can channel the embodiment of the visage to the extent they experience a short transformation. This would typically last for the ritual's duration, but those exceptionally disciplined could hold the form longer or invoke it anytime they wore the mask.

The twins centered their entire focus around the masks and unlocking the transformative power held within. They used what they'd already learned to hypnotize their parents into mindless zombies, and the girls stayed home from school for weeks practicing and perfecting. They laid claim to the boxed items and moved them to the basement, where they spent hours changing themselves back and forth between wolf and human until it became easy, natural.

The twins grew comfortable and confident In their abilities and desired to do what was necessary to take them to the next level. They needed to bring outsiders into their sanctuary, not as guests, but as sacrifices, so their culling of the neighborhood began, which unfortunately included Benny.

Despite the intense, fiery pain threatening to rip him apart, Benny found himself within reach of the banister just before his feet were taken out from under him. Something soft and lumpy broke his fall, but the momentum sent him sliding on his chest across the floor through thick, wet slime.

He rolled onto his back and propped himself up on his elbows but couldn't see what he'd tripped over until the twin wolves approached, burning black candles in hand. The light fell on what appeared to be a dirty pile of clothes and blankets, but then he saw Marcus's shredded, disfigured face peeking through the folds.

Deep gashes ran down the right side of Marcus's face, and his eyeball was missing from the ravaged empty socket. The left eye remained intact, wide open, and frozen in a permanent terror-stricken gaze. Everything below his nose had been violently sliced into jagged ribbons of flesh that hung unevenly across clenched white teeth visible through gaps in the grotesquely macabre beaded curtain.

Benny recognized torn remnants of the *White Sox* t-shirt Marcus frequently wore, as it had been the source of many disagreements between the two regarding team loyalty. The blanket he was wrapped in was large tufts of cotton turned pink with blood stuck to the boy's jumbled pieces, and the slimy substance he'd slid through was a mixture of his bodily fluids.

His elbows began to slide backward, and he tried to prop himself back up but found his arms were significantly shorter and covered in the same cotton-like substance Marcus was wrapped in. The wolves laughed, and one of them released a short but piercing howl. Benny didn't know what to do except scream, only it came out as a bleating wail. The steadily approaching twins erupted again in freakish laughter as Benny's repeated attempts to cry out yielded the same results.

He looked from the cackling wolves to Marcus's crumpled form and then back down at his body. Not only had the twins transformed themselves, but they'd also transformed Marcus and him. The white and pink tufts weren't cotton but wool, as they'd both been turned to sheep just like the mask they'd been made to wear.

The creatures Jessica and Pauline had become stood directly over Benny, and he felt the warm drops of drool falling from their fantastically fanged jowls.

"I think he just figured out the surprise," Jessica said to her sister.

"I think he did." Pauline crouched over Benny's small, quivering form to whisper in one of his newly placed ears. "I told you it would be fun."

They fell upon him using claws and teeth to tear chunks from his newly transformed body, delivering intense suffering to the little lamb. As Benny let go, he heard the desperate bleating of a sheep off in the distance until a droning wall of white noise smothered him into oblivion. ☠

I. SMUDGEFACE

I arrived at the bar early, as is my custom whenever I meet up with someone I matched with on *Tinder*. It helps me to feel more comfortable and more relaxed with the situation. I have time to settle in, become familiar with my surroundings, and have a pre-date drink or two to settle my nerves. I visited the bar bathroom first to check myself out, which is a compulsion of mine when I go on these dates, but it is all part of my ritual.

The bathroom was intentionally dark since everyone looked fantastic in low light, especially while drinking, but I had a solution. I used the flashlight on my phone to illuminate the space over the sink, preventing any of my features from being hidden by shadows. The smudge on my face was still there but hardly visible, even with the additional light. I wouldn't even call it a smudge since it was more of a smear and looked like it could be easily rubbed off by the spit-dampened hanky of an overbearing mother.

Still, it was there, and I'd have to work with it for now. I got nervous before these dates and hoped the smear wouldn't ruin my chances. I couldn't do anything now, so I decided it was best not to think about it and have a drink. I just have to hope my date can see past my imperfections and like me for who I am.

I pocketed my phone and stepped away from the mirror so I would stop obsessing about it. When I walked back out to the bar, I stayed in the shadow of the hallway and scanned the room to ensure my date hadn't decided to show up early like myself. It didn't take long to determine she wasn't there yet. According to her picture, she was incredibly striking, and no amount of dim bar light could mask her beauty.

I stepped up to the bar and ordered a whiskey neat, hurriedly drank it in two sips, and ordered another. The second was to sip before my date arrived, but I needed the first initial rush to help me relax. Usually, it worked like a charm, but relaxing was not in the cards for me this time. The shock of booze to my system only made me think about how horrible this date could become. The girl, her name was Elaine, according to her profile, was incredibly out of my league. The fact we matched and she agreed to go out with me required some suspension of disbelief on my part.

Still, I had plenty of friends with significant others who, on the surface, did not seem to go with each other. Being a positive kind of guy with really nothing to lose, I decided to take the chance. The worst thing that could happen was she didn't show, or she did but turned around and walked out upon seeing me. My mother always told me, 'Nothing ventured, nothing gained', which is usually true, but to an extent. There should be addendums to anecdotal advice, such as, 'Nothing ventured, nothing added to your already low self-worth and body image issues', but I guess that's too wordy and doesn't roll off the tongue so well.

I still had ten minutes until our agreed-upon meeting time, and I debated another drink. I absently brushed my hand against the smear on my face, and the decision was made for me. I placed the glass on the bar and motioned to the bartender for a refill. I took a small sip, put it on the bar, and took out my phone, hoping the distraction would keep me drinking too quickly. I absently opened *Tinder* and brought up Elaine's profile, even though I'd looked at it a dozen times before coming to the bar.

I scanned the short bio I'd read repeatedly, hoping to glean something new about my date. There are some hidden details I could connect with her on and use to keep her interested long enough to get to know me a little better. Of course, this was all contingent on whether my appearance sent her sprinting in the opposite direction before I could speak.

The bio revealed nothing again, and I quickly looked through the few pictures on her profile before closing the app and shoving my phone into my pocket. I didn't need a reminder of how ultra-desirable and utterly out of my league this woman was, so I went to take another quick sip of my drink but instead poured the remainder of the glass down my throat.

The liquor worked quickly to beat back my rising self-consciousness and imbue me with a sudden and uncharacteristic boost of confidence. I didn't need to feel bad about the way I looked. Who cares if hardly anyone swipes on my picture? The important thing is that Elaine did; she was coming to meet me right here. Looks aren't everything to everybody. Different strokes for different folks, and such, and the like.

"Excuse me, are you Carl?"

The voice came from behind, and when I turned around, my newfound confidence drained completely. It was Elaine, and she was unbelievably more desirable in person than in her pictures. Her features had been perfectly smudged across her face from constant swiping, so much so the difference between them was indistinguishable. I stared at her but could not tell where the voice she had spoken to me with came from. The edges of her face were pulled away from the center in mismatched, uneven swaths of flesh like large globs of Silly Puddy teased out to different lengths.

Some areas had been worked over more than others, with smudges pushed out farther in those places and blurred around the edges. Her hair, as well as the rest of her face, was all smudged to the right. Most of her face had been swiped into her hair, which I could only assume was originally blonde, but there was no way to tell now. I thought I saw an eye peeking behind what looked like bangs, but it was just a trick of the dim bar lights.

Elaine had obviously been swiped right on countless times, and her face had become a surrealist painter's wettest of dreams. I pictured her face dripping from the side of a steep ridge or bare tree branch in some fantastical Dali creation kept safe on the wall where it hung sectioned off by red velvet ropes to keep admirers six feet back from the masterpiece.

I reached up, rubbed the tiny, almost imperceptible smudge on my cheek, and then flushed crimson with embarrassment. Elaine continued staring at me, and I could only imagine her smudged and rearranged face was emoting confusion.

"Carl?" she asked again. "Are you Carl? I mean, you are Carl, right? At least you look like the picture on his profile."

She held up her phone and gestured toward me with it. I went to answer, but the words stuck in my throat and the buzz I had accrued while waiting began to rapidly diminish.

"I'm . . . uh, I'm . . ."

I couldn't speak, stunned by her otherworldly beauty. It was as if she had somehow reached down my throat and squeezed my vocal cords to keep them from operating correctly. I looked down at the dingy bar floor, attempting to break her spell over me, and it partially worked. I could speak again, but not at all intelligibly.

"Carl? Who? Me? No. Not Carl." The words fell from my mouth like clunky, jagged, mismatched bricks not meant to fit together.

"Oh," she said, sounding somewhat genuinely disappointed. "My mistake. You just look so much like his picture, and I thought—"

"Yeah, I get that a lot," I said, rising from the stool and pushing past her, still refusing to look back at her mesmerizing beauty. "Excuse me, I have to be going now. Good luck finding your friend."

I hurried past her, keeping my head down, pushed through the door, and stepped out on the sidewalk in the cool night air. I zipped my coat and pulled my collar tight against my neck to keep the biting wind away. I began walking toward my apartment, wallowing in my own self-defeat.

I don't know why I kept doing this to myself. I was no good at dating and was foolish to think an app would change that. I plunged my hands deep into my pockets and buried my chin into my chest as I walked so that no passersby could see how ugly I was.

A minute later, I felt the soft vibration of my phone against my chest from my inner breast pocket. At the same time, I felt a sharp pressure against the center of my face, followed by the sound of someone punching wet dough. I reached up to touch my face and couldn't help but smile. My nose was considerably flatter than it was moments ago and had been pushed down at an angle to the right of my mouth. My left eye was also now considerably lower and had shifted to the center of my face, closer to where my nose had originally been.

I ripped my jacket open and snatched my phone to confirm my suspicion. The vibrating notification I'd felt resulted from a *Tinder* match and what I hoped would be the start of the rest of my face smudged and smeared to the right.

I pulled my collar and proudly held my head up from my chest as I checked my phone, hoping people would take notice of my newly swiped appearance. The girl who'd matched with me was Natalie, and according to her picture, she was slightly more smudged than me. I swiped right, adding to her blossoming beauty, and immediately messaged her to see if she was available to meet up this evening.

I walked as I typed, growing more confident with every step. Natalie was free and agreed to meet at a bar only a few blocks away in an hour. I ran my fingers across my newly arranged face and smiled as I walked to the bar. Maybe tonight wouldn't be a total loss after all. ☠

CURSE OF THE DEAD CENTER

ursed." The man's voice was loud but nonchalant. "Whole place is cursed."

Terry could hear them shout before getting out of his truck.

"Grounds' cursed too; don't waste your time."

In all the years Terry Sullivan had been a developer, he hadn't had nearly as much trouble with a property as with this one. At a glance, it was a partially burned-out shack sitting at an odd angle to the ground because it had halfway sunk into a massive hole beneath. The opening was lined with jagged edges of charred wood and busted cement, deterrents from the twisted black mess below where the fire had been its angriest.

It used to be a club, a rock club, or, more appropriately, a *punk* rock club. At least, in the end, it was. Places like *The Dead Center* usually take a while to get on their feet and find their identity, only it seemed to find it faster than most. It started as a dirty beer bar with a small stage in the corner graced mostly by wannabe singer/songwriters with too much moxie and too little talent. The only standout in the bunch was a kid who went by Tony Fink.

He couldn't sing or play guitar well at all, not at first. Some say he never did, but they were jealous. He had passion and grit, two things painfully absent from others attempting to launch their star from the same triangular-shaped platform in the dark corner of that bar.

He called himself *That Finkelstein Shit Kid* when it was just him, a nod to a movie most people listening to his music hadn't seen but still amused by the wordplay. When he put the band together, the name changed briefly to *Those Finkelstein Shit Kids* and then to *Those Shit Kids* before settling simply on *Shit Kids.* They were always billed as *Tony Fink and the Shit Kids* though the name was never officially changed until after the fire, and even then, hardcore fans didn't recognize the modification. It would always be *Shit Kids* to them.

This wasn't the kind of thing Terry was interested in. He couldn't give a shit less about some shitty band's legacy or whatever their handful of trashy braindead 'fans' had to say about them. He wanted to make money and move on but couldn't do that with Tony Fink's supporters refusing to leave the property.

This was gonna be the last time he came out here to talk, though this was the last conversation before the police were brought in to remove them forcibly. Terry didn't want it to come to that. He didn't want there to be a scene. This was why he headed straight for the person who had some semblance of control over the group, the one they would listen to.

Tony's brother, Frank, sat six feet to the right of the hole in his usual spot. His portable canvas camping chair had seen better days, and from the looks of Frank, so had he. The bottom half of his belly hung like a waxing crescent moon from the bottom of his ill-fitting *Shit Kids* shirt. His hair was an unkempt, wild tangle of brush atop his head, and a tall can of Pabst Blue Ribbon beer clutched in his right hand. A small Styrofoam cooler with more of the same sat on the ground next to him.

This wasn't his first encounter with Frank, who was, in fact, who filled him in on the story of Tony and *The Dead Center.* He referred to it as *The Dead,* along with the other creepy fans who skulked the property day and night like it was their job to keep people from getting in or something else from getting out. It was hard to communicate with them because they mainly spoke in broken sentences peppered liberally with lyrics from *Shit Kids* songs, but Terry felt he had a good chance of getting through to Frank.

"Cursed," Frank said when Terry was within ten feet of the hole. "Place is cursed. Best just to move along."

"Hey there, Frank," Terry said, approaching Frank's chair, his throne. "I know about the curse. You told me, remember? It's me, Terry. You told me the whole story about a week ago about your brother and—this place."

Frank stared and said nothing as he swigged from the beer can, showing no sign of recognition toward the developer. Terry waited another moment, but Frank drank again, deeply, tipping the can up until it was empty. He tossed it into the hole and reached for another from the cooler.

"So, you know then," he said, pulling the tab on his fresh PBR. "Good."

"Yeah, good," Terry said, burying his hands in his pockets and kicking at the dirt. "And I'm sorry about your brother Frank, really sorry. I know how it hurts to lose someone so close to you."

It was a lie. Terry had never lost anyone close to him.

"Thing is," he continued, "we all have to move on sometime, and I hate to say it, but I think it's that time for you and your— friends—"

Terry gestured to the small clusters of people posted at different spots around the property in canvas chairs of their own, beers in hand. Frank looked confused, then hurt before his eyes showed the emotion they expressed best: anger.

"We can't," Frank replied simply, sipping his beer again. "We can't *move on*. We can't leave, and you can't stay. The cur—"

"Yeah, yeah, the curse. I know." Terry was pacing now, trying to keep his frustration from showing. "You told me, but the thing is, this property has been bought by my company, and we need to start working. I promise we'll be respectful to the memory of your brother. Maybe we can have a plaque put up or some—"

"Is this a joke to you?" Frank was standing now; his fresh beer lay beside the chair, spilling into the dirt and grass. "Do you think we made this up? That we're *crazy* or something?"

"Now Frank, I didn't mean to imp—"

"Do you understand what a curse is? How it works? He cursed us. He cursed us all, this whole place!"

"*Who* cursed you?"

Terry regretted asking the moment the question left his mouth but thought allowing Frank to explain might deescalate the situation.

"Tony," Frank said. "My brother. He couldn't leave well enough alone, couldn't just be satisfied. He had to push it. He wanted more, and he got it. Now, we're all paying the price."

This was the first time it occurred to Terry that these people could *actually* be dangerous. It was evident whatever the curse was about, they believed in it wholeheartedly. Frank's vehemence was intimidating.

"That music, *his* music, he called it. It all started with that." Frank was rocking from side to side now but didn't make eye contact with the developer. "He said he owed his success to the sacrifices he'd made, not the kind you think. But he needed more. Always more and more sacrifices. He was out of control."

"Sacrifices?"

"They were for whoever he'd gone into business with, his partner, he called them, only they were calling more of the shots than Tony. I loved my brother too much to let it keep going on. That's why we had the fire."

"Wait, wait," Terry stumbled. "Are you saying *you* started the fire that burned the club down and—killed your brother."

"It was less about killing him and more about stopping *it*, what he was becoming. We had to trap it to save Tony. It was the only thing we could do at that point."

Frank stooped to pluck another beer from the cooler, and, feeling their eyes on him, Terry turned to find everyone on the property intently watching him. Beers in hand, silent, staring. Something wasn't right. His truck was parked fifty feet away but might as well have been fifty miles. He fought an overwhelming urge to run, sprint to the truck, take off, and let the cops deal with this mess of crazies.

The sea of cold, blank stares operated like a barrier that kept him from acting on the impulse. He didn't think they'd let him get too far.

"Look, Frank," Terry started. "I think this is just a misunderstanding. I'm going to go back and talk with my bosses to see if we can do some—"

"The only bad thing to come out of the whole mess was the curse. Son-of-a-bitch got it out at the last possible second. Otherwise, we wouldn't be having this conversation."

Terry took a step back. He didn't like how Frank spoke now. His tone and inflection have gone dark. What was he thinking coming out here by himself to try and persuade a group of burnout psycho-squatters to 'kindly move along'? He should've called the police from the start. Too bad should'ves don't mean shit when it's already too late.

"Frank, I want you to—"

"We are," Frank continued. "Having this conversation, I mean. It's unfortunate, but we can do nothing about it now. We just have to keep it going so Tony stays safe, so *it* doesn't get out."

He gestured over his shoulder to the hole behind him, and Terry took another step back.

"So, you see, we can't leave. We're bound by responsibility. It's our duty. If we fail, none of what Tony did matters anymore; he gave too much for that to happen. The sacrifices must continue. For Tony. For the *Shit Kids*."

Terry turned to run but was stopped by a wall of Tony's dirty faithful, standing directly behind him, blocking his escape route. Their dead eyes fixed into malevolent stares rimmed in a dull orange glow. Somewhere in the background, over their heads, he saw the flames. His truck was on fire.

He spun back around and found Frank had closed the gap between them. It happened fast. Terry was already falling before he realized Frank had grabbed his arm and flung him toward the gaping burned-out maw, the hole his brother died in. No, the hole he *killed* his brother in.

It was where the curse started, and as Terry fell face first, hurling toward scorched remains of what equated to love and death, he understood. ☠

FAMILY VACATION OR PERIL ON THE HIGH SEA

Gillian loathed spending time with her family. The small, day-to-day segments in which she was forced to do so was one thing, but spending every waking second with them for five days straight was going to be absolutely insufferable.

Where did her father get off thinking he could make her endure something so torturous when the thought of spending time with her family made her physically ill. Twice! Gillian actually puked two times just thinking about it since her father made the announcement over dinner, which was one of the unfortunately required segments of time Gillian was forced to endure with her mother, father, and younger siblings, who were paternal twins.

The twins' names were Brian and Brianna, who were eight years old. Gillian hated their names as much as she hated everything else about them.

It was unceremonious and matter of fact and said between passing the steamed asparagus and a plate of what Gillian's mother called 'browned meat'.

"I've found myself with some time off from work," her father said flatly, accepting a dish with one hand while passing one off with the other. "So, we're going on vacation together. A family vacation."

His last two words, 'family' and 'vacation' hit Gillian like a one-two punch delivered point-blank by a cannon. She was so stunned. In fact, she went temporarily deaf for the next three to five seconds. Her hearing slowly returned, but she quickly wished it had gone again as her ears filled with the awful squeals of her brother and sister, an indication of their delight.

Gillian leapt from her seat and rushed down the hall to the bathroom. This was the first time she became ill over what a 'family vacation' meant. She puked until nothing came out but still heaved like she was practicing for an impending eating disorder.

She returned to the table amidst excited chatter about the terrible thing her father had said, most of it coming from the twins. Her mother smiled as her father nodded along with her sibling's jabbering when Gillian sat back down. Nobody noticed she'd been gone.

"And we can swim with the dolphins!" Brian exclaimed.

"And ride a jet ski, sailboat, and speedboat, and a—" Brianna would've kept going if her father hadn't cut her off.

"Yes, yes," he said, scooping a large helping of scalloped potatoes onto his plate. "We can do all of that. I don't know about the speedboat, but we'll do *most* of those things. We have five whole days!"

Gillian felt the burning bite of bile creep back up her throat again. She told herself he didn't say 'five whole days'; he said 'may-o-naise' or 'fly-a-ways'. Gillian wished more than anything she could fly away from the table and never come back.

"You've been awfully quiet, Gill," her mother said as if she just realized her first-born child was sitting at the table. "What do you think? Aren't you excited to go to Mexico?"

Her father must have revealed their destination while Gillian was either briefly deaf or in the bathroom because this was the first she'd heard it. Also, she hated it when her mother called her *Gill*; even worse, her mother *knew* she hated it. Gillian thought she might be trying to playfully pick on her by constantly shortening the name, but lately, she'd started to believe her mom was just plain dumb.

"Excited?" Gillian said the word like it was the first time she'd heard it out loud. "I wouldn't use that word to describe how I feel."

"I know, me too," her mother said between forkfuls of browned meat. "I would have to say I feel . . . ecstatic!"

Gillian looked across the table into her mother's glassy eyes briefly, considering she possibly suffered a mild form of brain damage.

"I don't think we're talking about the same thing, Mom," she said.

Gillian's mother smiled. She had browned meat stuck between her teeth.

"Come on, kiddo," Gillian's father said while the twins chatted mindlessly amongst themselves. "It's gonna' be a blast hanging with your old man and the rest of the crew, and a little sun wouldn't kill you. Would it?"

Gillian was fair-skinned and paler than most other fourteen-year-old girls who attended her school. She only wore black, and the contrast added more of a ghostly touch to her complexion. To be honest, Gillian was fairly positive a *little sun* could and most likely *would* kill her, but that was not the hill she wanted to die on right now.

"What about the cartels?" Gillian asked, blowing past the whole 'sun' debate. "I saw on the news it's not safe to go to Mexico right now because of them."

This shut both twins up at the exact moment like someone had simultaneously pulled their plugs. They looked wide-eyed from Gillian to their father, waiting for him to assuage their fear. He scoffed with a mouthful of potato, sending partially chewed bits across the table where they dotted the untouched food on Gillian's plate like a regurgitated garnish.

"Pahrpasaras!" He exclaimed, repeating for clarity once he'd swallowed his food. "Preposterous! The news only says those kinds of things to get ratings. Maybe one guy a long time ago was killed by the cartel because he tried to rip them off, and the news stations have been sensationalizing the whole story. They want you to be too scared to leave your home until they say it's safe to go outside again.

"Well, let me tell you something, Gillian, they ain't ever gonna' say it's safe to go anywhere because safety doesn't sell ad space! If it's not the cartels killing people, they'll tell you it's something else equally as unappealing, like the place is diseased or flooded, or even say the whole country's been overrun by zombies if it'll keep people tuned in!

"Besides, those kinds of things only happen in border towns anyway. We'll be perfectly safe at the resort."

The twins jolted back to life at the mention of a resort. They both started asking different questions at the same time, turning the expression of their renewed excitement into unintelligible gibberish.

Gillian's father filled his mouth with more from the mess on his plate, turned his attention to the twins, and smiled as he nodded like he could understand what they were saying. Gillian's mother cast big, dead doe-eyes toward her husband while chewing behind an empty smile. Gillian couldn't tell if she agreed with him or following the sound.

"We're going to a resort?" Gillian slipped the question in between her sibling's jabbering.

"That's right." He looked over at Gillian's mother, squeezed her arm, and mimicked her smile. "An *all-inclusive* resort just like we always talked about going one day. Isn't that right, darlin'?"

"Just. Like. It."

Each word lacked more commitment than the one before, but she never stopped smiling. Gillian didn't care about her mother's slightly less-than-normal behavior anymore because she was still reeling from distributing new information. Her sole concern was where she fit in amidst each new wrinkle her father doled out like the third helping of potatoes onto his plate.

"Doesn't that mean we'll be trapped on a small square of the beach until, hopefully, the shuttle bus guy you tipped twenty-bucks returns to get us in five days?"

"It means, Gillian, that we won't have to pay for food or drinks while there. We don't even have to tip!" Her father paused to cut a piece of meat, like not having to tip was some kind of accomplishment that deserved respectful reflection. "And we won't be *trapped,* Ms. Smarty Pants. There's plenty of beach to play on, plus with all the excursions we're taking out on the water, you won't have any time to be bored. Don't you worry about that."

The twins erupted again In high-pitched shrieks of jubilation, which proved too much for their father to take this time, and he raised his voice to calm them down.

"All right, all right, that's enough, Brian and Brianna," he said loudly but without the intonation of anger. "Let's save some of that excitement for the trip, okay kids."

They quieted down enough for Brianna to ask the question Gillian was about to ask herself.

"When do we leave, Daddy?"

"We fly out first thing Monday morning," their father answered, dumping the last helping of asparagus from the serving tray to his plate.

The twins squealed in unison, and Gillian cringed, bringing her hands to her ears to block as many decibels as possible. At any moment, she expected all the dogs in the neighborhood to start barking in response to the children's piercing wail.

"Quiet down, quiet down," their father said, having to yell to cut through the twins' expression of joy. "Why don't you kids play in your room or outside or something, huh?"

He kept the smile on his face, but Gillian could tell he was trying to hide the loss of his patience. Typically, the twins were made to remain at the table until they'd both cleaned their plates, and Gillian looked to her mother for an objection that did not come. Brian and Brianna leapt from their chairs and continued to scream with delight up the stairs to their room, mainly leaving full plates of food behind.

Gillian waited a few seconds before speaking, hoping some explanation or clarification would be offered up from one or both of her parents. Still, as they chew and smile, she decided to initiate.

"When you say Monday," Gillian started, "you meant the first Monday of summer vacation, right?"

"No, I mean this coming Monday."

He said it as if the line was being recited on a shitty primetime sitcom, but this was reality and a lot shittier. Gillian's mother continued to smile and chew, smile, and chew.

"But today is Thursday," Gillian said slowly.

"That's right."

"Monday is only three days away. Are you saying we're leaving on this . . . this— "

"Vacation," her father interjected.

"Yes, that. Are we leaving for *that* in three days? All of us?"

"Mm-hmm." He managed through a mouthful of meat.

"What about school? It's the middle of October?"

"So, you and the twins will miss a week of school." Gillian's father was gesturing with his fork to visually punctuate his words. "Is that so bad? When I was a kid, I would've loved it if the old man pulled me out of school for a week to go fishing."

Gillian waited for her mother to jump in and stop this insanity. She might have let it slide when the twins didn't clean their plates, but there was no way she would stand for all three of them missing an entire week of school.

"What about work, Dad? How can you take a week off on such short notice? Won't your boss be upset?"

"You don't need to worry about that. It's all been taken care of." Gillian's father wiped a napkin across his lips one final time before letting it drop to his empty plate. "Excellent dinner as always, sweetheart. Just fantastic."

He leaned over to kiss his wife on the forehead before pushing away from the table and standing. He turned and headed off to the living room, picking at the stringy bits of meat stuck between his teeth with his fingernail along the way. Gillian's mother stood, picked up the two plates, and took them to the kitchen, smiling without a word.

Gillian was left alone at the table. She hadn't taken a single bite of her dinner and didn't want to. She waited a few minutes for something else to happen, only didn't know what she was expecting. Maybe a purple elephant with angel wings would walk through the house, and she'd realize she was dreaming.

Maybe a sinkhole would open beneath the dining room to swallow Gillian and all her problems? When neither happened, she begrudgingly left the table, skulking to her room.

Later in the evening, Gillian heard her parents talking through the vent connecting her room to theirs, and while she didn't like what she heard, it cleared some things up. Her father had been fired from his job, explaining why they could leave so soon but not why they had to.

Gillian also learned her mother had just refilled her prescription for Xanax and was choosing to ignore the warnings about mixing it with alcohol. This explained her zombie-like behavior during dinner and why she didn't object to the kids missing school or show concern over losing her husband's job. Gillian didn't care about her father's job either, especially when compared to how she felt about the idea of spending five days with the four people she hated more in the world than anyone.

Gillian sloughed off her covers, quietly got out of bed, and retrieved the stack of books she kept hidden beneath a pair of fuzzy bunny slippers she had no intention of ever wearing. She took the books to her desk, turned on the lamp shaped like a black cat, and sat down.

The lamp was purchased with some of the money Gillian got when she returned the dress her parents gave her for her most recent birthday. It was a pink, ruffled, chiffon disaster, the only good thing being its cost. She skipped school one day to return the dress to the trendy store in the mall her parents bought it from and, to her delight, found she had enough money to buy the cat lamp and the books she'd wanted.

Gillian was serious about becoming a witch, although her parents and teachers seemed to think it was just a phase. She'd known since she was five years old and had been making vocal declarations of her intent ever since. Now that she'd finally gained access to some books on magic and witchcraft, Gillian felt ready to manifest her destiny.

The woman who ran the small occult bookstore in town smelled like cloves and dirty dreadlocks, but Gillian dealt with the unpleasant aroma long enough to purchase what she'd been coveting. There was one by Crowley, one on chaos magic, another on the basics of witchcraft and working within a coven, and the fourth was on minor spells and summoning.

The woman told her she wouldn't need the last book until she'd familiarized herself fully with the first three, but Gillian didn't have time for that. She would be thrust into her own personal hell in three days unless she could successfully pull off a magical miracle. Determined, she sat at her desk with the book on spells, pulled out a notebook from the top drawer, and started reading.

Gillian opened her eyes, having been ripped from a sound sleep by the bleating of her alarm clock from across the room. She lifted her head from the book she'd fallen asleep reading and was groggy but happy to be out of the nightmare she'd been having. All she remembered was being stuck in a small, dark space like a closet; her entire family was with her.

It was pitch dark and moist, with only enough room for the five to fit without an inch to spare. Gillian screamed but could make no sound and tried to thrash herself free to no avail. She could only wait as the air ran out, and they all died. Together. It was the worst possible fate she could imagine.

Gillian left her room hoping to get into the bathroom before the twins invaded it, but when she passed their open door, they were sitting on the floor between their beds, surrounded by toys, playing a bastardized version of *Candyland.*

"Hey, Gillian!" Brian called out.

"Hey, Gillian!" Brianna echoed.

"Did Dad tell you?" Asked Brian.

"Yeah, did Dad tell you," His sister parroted.

"Tell me what?" Gillian was suddenly very interested. "Is the vacation canceled?"

"No, silly," Brian continued. "He said we don't have to go to school today!"

"We get to stay home and get ready for the trip," Brianna said, holding up a plush unicorn. "I'm packing my toys right now."

As much as Gillian didn't like staying home all day with her family, not going to school would give her extra time to study her spells.

"Where is dad anyway?" She asked, glancing over her shoulder at her parents' closed bedroom door.

"He went to get donuts!" Brian squealed, pumping both fists like he had just won something.

"He said to be quiet because mommy needed her sleep," Brianna added.

"Yeah, I bet she does," Gillian muttered.

"What?" The twins asked in unison.

"Nothing," she said quickly. "Tell Dad I'll be in my room and *don't* want to be bothered. Also, I don't think it matters how much noise you make. I have a feeling Mommy could sleep through an earthquake right now."

With that, Gillian turned on her heel and returned to her room. Her father disturbed her when he returned home with donuts, blaming his intrusion on wanting to make sure the twins 'gave me the message.' She told him they did but had clearly not given him *her* message. Gillian refused his offer of donuts but did ask for some coffee, which he reluctantly provided.

"Just don't tell your mother," he said, closing the door behind him.

After studying all day, Gillian suffered through a short dinner, shoveling chunks of the bland, frozen chicken potpie her father had only semi-cooked. Most of the inside was cool, and some bits of carrots and peas were even still frozen. Gillian didn't comment or complain, not wanting anything to keep her at the table one second longer than necessary.

"I'm done," she announced through a mouthful of lukewarm slop. "Going back upstairs to study for the week of school I'll miss."

"That a girl," Gillian's father called after her. "Get it done now so you won't have to worry about it while we're on vacation!"

Her stomach lurched at mentioning the word 'vacation', and Gillian doubled her pace to make it to the bathroom before she became physically ill for the second time. The potpie exited her system almost as fast as she'd gobbled it down, and after a quick gargle of mouthwash, Gillian was back in her room at her desk, hoping to learn a spell to stop the trip from happening.

By Sunday afternoon, she wasn't any closer to figuring out how to make her magic work and was starting to get desperate. She was particularly discouraged to find the type of summoning she wanted to perform required 'nothing less than human blood', which she recorded into her notebook word for word. That meant she couldn't cheap out using the juice from raw meat or any other animal.

Unfortunately, it was too late for Gillian to do anything with the information by the time she'd discovered it. She briefly considered slitting one of the twins' throats but figured it would be more trouble than it was worth. It was simply too late, and Gillian was too exhausted to read anymore, but she wasn't ready to give up.

She may not have been able to stop the vacation, but she still had a chance to significantly shorten its length with a properly timed spell. At least that's what Gillian hoped as she hid her books and notes underneath the clothes in her suitcase before falling into a deep sleep.

She remembered traveling to the resort in brief flashes, much like a blackout drunk might recall events from the prior evening. She was so tired and slept so heavily as they traveled it felt like she blinked her eyes and suddenly found herself in a small hotel room on a Mexican beach.

Between glimpses of reality, she dreamed of being stuck in the cramped darkness with her family. It repeated over and over, resetting each time she briefly awoke and fell back asleep. Despite the awful dreams and disorienting arrival, Gillian felt well-rested with a renewed drive.

Her father was rushing the family out the door for their first of many scheduled excursions, but she retrieved the spell book from her suitcase and slipped it into her small backpack. A couple of life-jackets and signed waivers later, Gillian and the rest of her family were on a small boat piloted by two guides whose job was to show them dolphins.

Her mother, father, and the twins stood against the railing, watching the water rush by while Gillian sat beneath what little shade there was and went back to reading. If there was a spell to cut the vacation short that didn't require human blood, she was determined to find it.

"Look! Look!" Brian called, pointing out into the ocean.

"It's a dolphin! Look, Mommy, it's a dolphin," Brianna shouted, grabbing her mother's hand. "It's a big dolphin!"

"Uh, kids," Gillian heard her father say. "I don't think that's a dolphin. In fact, a senior is that—"

The guides were manning the small motor at the rear of the boat and suddenly started speaking excitedly in Spanish. Gillian didn't know exactly what they were saying but knew enough to know something was wrong.

Something bad.

She turned to face them but saw them looking past where her family was standing. Their faces were colorless and frozen in fear. Gillian turned back around just in time to see the top half of a massive shark breach the surface. The beast snatched Brian from the boat's edge with a mouth like a giant hole filled with teeth. Two sneakered feet attached to jagged stumps were all left of him, and then there was the blood.

There was a lot of blood.

Chaos erupted across the boat, but Gillian remained calm and stood holding the book out in front of her, already open to the page she'd marked. She had the blood, and while she didn't have any candles, sage, or salt, Gillian hoped its abundance would make up for their absence. She tuned out the shrieks and screams of her family and the guides and focused on the words.

"In Hoc Sanguinem, Et vocavi vos, Ad extremum petere quod ad mandatum meum!"

Gillian shouted, trying to enunciate and be heard over the screaming. She didn't have time to practice beforehand and struggled to pronounce Latin words she'd never heard aloud. A beat passed, and then another.

Gillian's father was leaning over the already low railing, screaming Brian's name into the growing patch of red in the water. Her mother hyperventilated, staring down at Brian's bloody stumps, her hands clutching at her chest, while Brianna bawled uncontrollably, calling for her mommy.

Then, there was a split second of silence where everyone breathed in unison, and within that small moment, Gillian felt it.

One of the guides muttered something in Spanish about *el Diablo*, but Gillian didn't turn around. Her eyes remained fixed on the sharp, gray fin slicing smoothly through the choppy black water as they returned to the boat. As morbid as it was, Gillian had never seen such an accurate depiction of the phrase 'hot knife through butter'. Only in this example the knife could be replaced by a samurai sword or a battle-axe.

The terrifyingly fast-approaching calling card appeared the size of a car door until the shark broke the surface again, revealing the lower half of the pre-historic appendage. This time, Gillian looked better at the monster as its massive maw clamped down around her father. Its teeth sliced through the ever-expanding paunch of his dad-bod with all the delicateness of a band saw cutting tissue paper.

The shark didn't bite completely through his midsection but instead pulled him off the boat, where his legs flailed from its mouth like the wind-powered waving cylinders of fabric at a car dealership designed to grab your attention from the highway. The shark opened its mouth enough for the rest of Gillian's father's body to slip through before disappearing beneath the water again.

The sound of Gillian's mother's head hitting the deck after she fainted was loud enough to be heard over the frenzied screams of the two guides and the perma-bawling of her little sister. Gillian smiled and looked back down at the book. It was working.

Wasn't it?

"*Tenebricosae sectae,*" Gillian continued reading from the book, but she didn't have to be as loud to be heard this time. "*Dominatus praepotens aurubis percipite verba mea!*"

Thunder sounded far away, but no clouds were in the sky.

Brianna moved toward her unconscious mother's body but made it only a single step before slipping in the comingled blood of her father and brother. The lone twin put her hands out to try and brace the fall, but her palms could find no purchase on the slick deck. Her head hit the floor harder than her mother's, only the noise wasn't as loud.

One of the guides pushed past Gillian as Brianna's tiny ragdoll form started sliding across the deck on its way to the edge. The panicking man leapt over the girl's mother, but his back foot caught the top of her shoulder, shifting his momentum downward. His chest hit the deck just as the little girl's body slipped beneath the flimsy railing and into the sea with the minimalized splash of an Olympic diver.

Gillian figured an obnoxiously fanged gaping deathtrap would be waiting to catch her troll of a sister. Still, when it didn't immediately happen, she silently cursed herself for not reading the words faster. A few moments passed without additional activity, and Gillian looked back to the book to see if she'd skipped something or misread one of the words.

The tripped guide pushed himself to his knees and started crawling his way back toward Gillian. The guide who remained behind heard her reading from the book and suspected she had something to do with what was happening but didn't know how to stop it. He knew she scared him almost as much as the shark she may or may not be manipulating.

A small eruption of air bubbles finally signified the child's demise, punctuated by the crimson cloud that floated to the surface and quickly spread out to become part of the bloody ring surrounding the boat. The shark's fin rose from the surf within six feet of the small vessel's starboard side, and Gillian heard the breath of the man behind her catch in his throat.

The fin slipped beneath the water, and a moment later, the boat rocked violently from being sideswiped by the enormous creature. Gillian steadied herself against the support beam of the eve she stood under while clutching the book tight against her chest. The gray and white beast looked bigger each time it surfaced, appearing more like a sea monster than a shark.

The boat shook again, but this time, the impact came from the port side with considerably more force behind it. Gillian held tight while the guide, who'd crawled over on his knees, now lay in the fetal position, his hands over his ears, repeating the Lord's Prayer in Spanish. The guide behind her clutched the wheel to keep from losing his footing, knowing one misstep would send him right over the railing.

The shark hit the side of the boat a third time, and both guides screamed out as Gillian realized what it was doing. The creature tried to rock the boat enough to slide her mother's unconscious body across the deck and into the water. Gillian watched the fin make its way around the ship's bow and made her move.

The boat was still rocking, so she took her steps carefully but quickly. When she reached her mother, Gillian tucked the book up high under her left arm, crouched next to the body, and pushed. She didn't bother to check if her mother was alive first.

It didn't take much effort to move the body since the deck was slick with blood and viscera, and Gillian could launch her mother toward the edge with the ease of pushing a stone across a frozen pond. The woman's momentum slowed as she approached the bow, and the body stopped several feet short of the water.

Gillian stood with a huff, intending to finish the job, but as she did, there was an explosion of water from the front of the boat. For a moment, she thought they were being fired upon by an enemy vessel, or maybe a rescue boat was trying to shoot the shark, but she hadn't seen another boat. The giant wall of water parted to reveal the cause.

The shark launched itself, having employed its massive capacity for propulsion, bringing gallons of seawater down on the deck a second before the entire front half of the humungous animal. The flimsy railing crumbled and may as well have been made of tinfoil for as much good as it did.

The sudden weight addition tipped the ship's bow down, and the guide at the wheel cried out for his god to save him as the port side rose several feet off the water into the air. Gillian stumbled forward but could somehow redistribute her weight quickly enough to remain upright. The book was still safely tucked under her arm. She took it out and held it with both hands as she watched the body easily slide the remaining distance to a waiting mouth.

The shark's cavernous jaws opened and closed in anxious anticipation, and having claimed its prize, the monster slid back off the boat into the bloody water. Pink and red waves lapped at the sides from the sudden and intense activity, and as the water began to settle, Gillian scanned the area for any sign of the shark.

She wasn't ready to jump for joy yet, but she was on the verge of extreme giddiness, which gave way to giggles she didn't try to suppress. It worked. She'd done it. It may have been messier than anticipated, but the desired result was achieved.

The vacation was undoubtedly over now, with the added bonus of not having to spend only five days with her family; Gillian would never have to spend time with them again.

She looked down at the book in her hands and then back out over the ocean, satisfied with having successfully taken her first steps down the left-hand path. She hugged the book of spells to her chest, anxious to learn what else it had to teach, excited to sharpen and hone her newfound skill for magic.

She heard the guide cry out a split second before his arms wrapped around her from behind. While one guide was still lying curled up on the deck, covering his ears, the other had decided to take matters into his own hands. He heard the girl reading from the book in a strange language, and he watched her push her mother's unconscious form into the mouth of their attacker. He refused to let himself be the next victim.

His only chance of survival hinged on removing the girl from the boat and doing it fast. He didn't hesitate in his approach for fear the girl could read his thoughts and would have time to use her powers to stop him. He ran from the rear of the boat despite the slippery conditions, wrapped Gillian in a bear hug from behind, pinning her arms to her sides, and picked her up.

Gillian dropped her book, and when it hit the deck, he kicked it hard enough to send it over the edge into the ocean. She held out a scream as long as her breath would allow, mainly for the loss of the book than her present predicament.

She kicked her feet wildly, trying to make contact with her captor's shins, or better yet, his groin, but the tight hold he had restricted the movement of her legs. She couldn't land a straight shot, and her attempts ended up glancing off the sides of the guide's legs.

"El Diablo! El Diablo! El Diablo!"

The man screamed the words into Gillian's ear as he walked her across the bow to the front of the boat, where the railing had been ripped off. She suddenly realized his intention and screamed for help to no one who cared.

"Not me! Not me! It's not supposed to work on me! Noooooo!"

As they approached the edge, Gillian saw a large ripple in the water, a split-second at a time, telegraphing her fate. The nose of the shark broke the surface, followed immediately by the wide-open fanged pit of death that was its mouth. The terrified guide stopped short and tossed Gillian over the side toward the opening like it was a game he'd been in training for his whole life.

She flailed uselessly, grabbing handfuls of air and falling head-first toward the waiting mouth. Gillian saw directly down the beast's throat where her family waited in its belly, and while some were in more pieces than others, most of her mother, father, and twins were accounted for.

Four pairs of milky dead eyes stared up at Gillian from faces she thought she'd never have to see again but would now be the last things she'd ever see. Never-ending rows of razor teeth carved deep lacerations into her back and legs as she fell into the shark's mouth. The shark swallowed her whole, and she slid down its salty, slick gullet to join her family.

The creature swam off, and as its belly filled with water, Gillian slowly drowned but was alive long enough to know her worst nightmare had come true. She would be forever trapped in a dark, cramped space with her family, never to escape.

Not even in death. ☠

SPEAKER SALE

"**H**ey buddy, you interested in some high-end speakers for cheap? I'll make you a great deal."

Shit! I was usually diligent about keeping my head on a swivel and staying aware of my surroundings when I pump gas, but a woman crossing the lot caught my attention. I wasn't being lecherous but was distracted because she and the dog she was walking had the same hairstyle. If I wasn't trying to figure out if it was on purpose, I would have spotted the guy before he got within six feet of me and waved him off.

Now, I was forced to interact with the skeezy, would-be conman up close and personal. The camera attached to the awning above me pointed directly at the pump I was using but did nothing to put me at ease. Most of the time, those things weren't hooked up at gas stations like this and were mostly for show in the hopes of acting as a deterrent.

The man with the supposed speakers had come around my car and leaned against the passenger side fender, hoping to put me at ease with his nonchalance. The scruff on his face looked like it hadn't seen the sharp end of a razor in over a week and sprouted from his chin in uneven patches of varied texture. It was like the guy's body gave up towards the end of puberty, leaving his adult characteristics mismatched and piecemeal.

His hair was cropped short, where it thinned across the top and wrapped around the sides and back in a horseshoe pattern. While the hair on his head and face was lacking, the hair in his ears was prosperous and plentiful. It exploded outward in wild salt-and-pepper colored tufts like streamers shot from a cannon during a ticker tape parade. The hair was so thick and knotted that I had no idea how sound waves could navigate through the small spaces between each strand to make it to the eardrum. The man chewed on a lit cigarette that dangled between thin, chapped lips.

"Do you really think you should be smoking next to a gas pump?"

I cursed myself for asking the question before I'd even finished. You're supposed to say 'no thank you' over and over until they leave. Now that I'd engaged him, he'd be much harder to shake.

"Ain't you heard that's an old wives tale? It's just a myth. We're perfectly safe." The man chuckled and took a long drag from his cigarette as if trying to illustrate his point.

"You think gas being highly flammable is a myth?"

I very badly wanted to pull the pump from my car and spray the man down to illustrate *my* point. Now that he and I were having a full-blown conversation, I knew disengaging would be near impossible. It was like we were playing chess, and I'd made a foolish first move that would have me playing defense the entire game.

"Look, pal, I'm no scientist," he said, managing to smile, showing all his piss-yellow teeth without the cigarette falling out. "Maybe you're right?"

The stranger plucked the cigarette from his mouth, exhaling the last bit of smoke still in his lungs, and flicked it off to the side, where it came to rest at the feet of a woman pumping gas across from us. She didn't notice because she was talking on her phone, another no-no while pumping gas as far as I was concerned.

"Yeah, maybe," I finally said, pulling my gaze from the smoldering butt. "Anyway, I'm not interested in any spea—"

"Look, friend, I understand," the man said, holding his hands out, a devilish smirk on his face, "but you haven't seen them yet. I mean, this is really legit shit, man. These speakers are only available to those in the music business or the ultra-rich audiophiles who know what music should sound like. "

I glanced over to see the numbers on the pump moving painfully slow, but that was how it typically went in the summer months, with more people than usual filling up at the same time. I still had a little more than half a tank to go.

"Well, I'm neither of those things," I said as a matter of fact as I could, "so I guess you have your answer right there."

"Yeah, well, who is these days really."

"I imagine plenty of music industry folk and rich audio-whatevers out there. Why else would they make speakers for a market that didn't exist?"

I was angry with myself for furthering the conversation with a question but was offended the guy would assume I was so dumb. Did I look that gullible? What is it that makes me seem like an easy mark? I must be doing something that screams approachability to people. Is it possible I'm not self-aware enough to know I displayed this particular trait?

"Here, why don't you at least take a look?"

The man quickly stepped behind my car and swung open the back doors of a white cargo van I hadn't noticed until now. It must have been there the whole time, which explains where the guy came from to begin with. The van was full of cardboard boxes stacked from floor to ceiling, all marked in black block letters with the word 'Speakers'.

No brand name, logo, or even fake brand names sounded like real ones like 'Sonay' or 'Magneticbox'. Normally, these guys would use the brand as an aggressive selling technique by telling you how much you're saving based on what the item goes for retail.

"Looks like I still don't need any speakers," I said as the pump mercifully stopped. "Thanks again."

I inserted the nozzle back into its holster on the side of the pump while pressing 'no' over and over on the keypad, waiting for the screen to ask if I needed a receipt. The shitty thing was I actually *did* need a receipt but couldn't wait the additional second it would take to print. I needed to get out now.

"Well," started the man, stepping closer as I reached for the door handle, "at least listen to what they sound like, and then make your decision."

The man gestured back toward the open van, and I stood on my toes to look over his shoulder at what he was referencing. There was about a foot of room between the bumper and where the stack of boxes started, and in that area sat the speakers in question. They were hooked up to micro versions of stacked stereo components.

"Look, I really don't have ti—"

I tried to sound stern but was interrupted by the opening to Led Zeppelin's *Immigrant Song* blasting from the van. The man hadn't moved, so I assume he'd triggered the song via remote control. I stood with my hand on my door handle, lingering as the crushing riff and driving beats of one of my favorite bands blasted in my face.

I hated to admit it, but the speakers had incredible clarity, especially at the volume they were being played, and a quality of realness I couldn't grasp. It sounded like I was in the studio listening to them record the song live. I was intrigued and let go of the door to look closer.

"I told you," the man said with a smile, flashing his police tape yellow teeth again. "Sounds great, right? Are you a Zeppelin guy?"

I took slow, purposeful steps toward the open van doors and listened hard to see if I could determine what stunt this guy was pulling that made these speakers sound too good to be true.

"They sound better than great," I said, trying to talk over the volume. "They sound incredible, and yes, I love Led Zeppelin."

The man stepped aside, allowing me a closer look at his wares, and the volume lowered to a point where we could talk over it comfortably but still hear the incredible clarity. He didn't touch the device to make this change. I imagined he had a remote small enough to fit into his pocket and pulled this routine with all potential buyers, enhancing the overall experience with an element of mystery.

I stood with my arms folded across my chest, examining the speakers and miniature stereo setup to which they were connected. I nodded to the music to cover that I was looking for any trace of fuckery involved in the demonstration. I looked for evidence of wires connected to other hidden speakers to boost the ones I looked at.

I stepped to the side to scan the seam between the carpet and the van wall but saw no trace of anything suspicious. I couldn't believe these could be the first pair of legitimate speakers sold out of the back of a van. I just couldn't. There was only one more thing I wanted to check before any price talk was brought up.

I uncrossed my arms, reached out, and picked up one of the speakers. The thing had significant weight for being small enough to palm, and my hand tingled from the vibration of bouncing cones within. Still, something felt odd about the speaker. The thing's weight was shifting in my hand like water would move in a bottle, but it wasn't a liquid-created sensation.

I gently rocked it and was reminded of what my Etch-A-Sketch felt like when I held it as a kid. I turned the speaker upside down, and the man moved to take it from me. Sand. The speaker was filled with sand. I shook it before the man ripped the speaker from my hand.

"I knew it was too good to be true," I said, shaking my head. "Good try, though. Better luck with the next sucker."

I pushed past him and swelled with satisfaction, knowing I wasn't as much of a gullible mark as I thought.

"Hey buddy, wait a minute," the man said, following behind with the speaker still in hand. "Just wait and let me explain."

My satisfaction was short-lived. I couldn't believe he had the gall to continue with his pitch as if he could explain away sand in the speaker. I whirled around to face him, and he stopped just short of running into me.

"Look," I started in the angry tone I reserved for yelling at cars in traffic from the safety of my own vehicle. "I don't know where you get off trying to push this fake shit on me, but I –"

"These aren't fake!" The man interrupted. "I'm telling you, listen. Let me explain something to you."

"Explain away, my friend, but you can tell it to my dust!"

I threw the car door open, plopped hard in the seat, slammed it behind me, and turned the key in the ignition.

The man leaned down to my open window and grabbed hold of the door to keep me from rolling it up.

"These speakers are *supposed* to be full of sand," he said desperately. "That's what gives them their unique—uh, qualities. See, it's still working just fine."

He pushed the speaker through the window and dropped it in my lap. The volume swelled suddenly, and the vibration rattled my groin with each mighty punch of John Bonham's kick drum. My mind wandered to an idea for a different speaker use for a split second, but I quickly pulled back from the thought.

"Yeah, so?" I shrugged, taking the speaker from my lap and handing it back through the window. "I'm sure they work great here with your special little setup, but the second I try to hook them up at home, they mysteriously fail, making me your number one gullible asshole of the day."

I tugged the shifter connected to the steering wheel into drive, but the man reached across and pulled it back into the park.

"Please," he said. "Just let me explain."

There was desperation in his tone that struck me as sincere. Maybe I was being an asshole to a guy trying to make an honest living? Against my better judgment, I turned off the ignition and stepped out of the car.

"Okay," I said, closing the door without slamming it behind me, "you have one minute to explain. If I'm still not interested, I leave without any more interference from you. Got it?"

The man smiled and nodded; a glint of canary yellow appeared briefly between his parted lips.

"If you'll just step back here with me, I'll be able to show you while I explain."

He stepped back toward the van's open doors with the speaker in one hand, gesturing me to follow with the other. I sighed heavily and strolled after him, my patience further thinning with each step. When I reached the back of the van, the man reached down, tapped the top of the miniature stereo, and the music stopped.

"You see this?" The man picked up a handful of sand from the pile I'd dumped out of the speaker and held it to my face.

"Yeah, yeah, I see it," I said, pushing his hand away. "I just poured it out a few seconds ago."

"I know, but look at it."

He brought it back to my face slower this time, and I reluctantly rolled my eyes down to take a look. There was something odd about the sand, something different. It looked much shinier than what you'd find at the beach, not sparkly but iridescent. Tiny swaths of magenta and deep crimson were also running through it.

"You see," he said, "this isn't just any normal sand. This is different, special. That's why it's *supposed* to be inside the speaker."

"I see." My tone was overly sarcastic. "So, what makes this sand so special?"

"It's . . . it's hard to explain, really," the man stammered, "but the sand is necessary for the full functionality of all the features."

A sudden change came over the man's demeanor. His confidence was beginning to waver, and tiny beads of sweat pushed through the pores above his lip and across his forehead.

"So, you mean to tell me the magic sand inside the speakers is required for? What did you say? Features? And what would these sandy *features* be?"

The man looked around as if we were having a conversation important enough for someone to eavesdrop on and leaned in close enough so I could smell his sour cigarette breath.

"The features are . . . special and unique. I'd really have to show you rather than explain."

"Well, that's kind of what I'm standing here waiting for," I fired off impatiently.

"Here," the man removed a small remote from his pocket, confirming my suspicion he'd been controlling the volume the whole time. "Take this."

I accepted the remote, which was smooth, black, and very plain. Four round pale blue buttons in the center sat flush with the housing. It felt like I was holding a polished stone. The man placed the speaker down where it had been before I picked it up and stepped back out of the way, leaving me facing the back of the van.

"Now," started the man, "close your eyes and press the button."

"Close my eyes? I don't think so, pal, and what button are you talking about? There are four of them."

"Fine, don't close your eyes," he huffed, "and just push any button."

I sighed again but was disappointed in myself for entertaining this entire exchange for so long. I was already this far, so I figured I might as well see it through. I lifted my arm, pointed it at the mini-stereo thing, and hit the top left button.

The opening of *Immigrant Song* played again at a significantly higher volume than earlier and shellacked my face with Robert Plant's piercing battle cry. It sounded amazing, and if the sand had something to do with it, the quality didn't suffer from missing what I'd dumped onto the van's floorboard. I did wish the guy had cued up a different song. I loved Led Zeppelin, but I'd like to hear how the speakers handled the low end of a hip-hop song or what orchestral music sounded like coming through these supposed 'high-end' speakers.

I realized I couldn't see my hand as the verse lyrics kicked in. I still hold my arm before me, pointing the remote at the device. At least it felt like I was, but now my hand, arm, and remote were gone. I felt disoriented and closed my eyes, pinched the brim of my nose, and took a step back to try and regain my bearings.

I brought my hand a few inches away from my face, held it there, and opened my eyes. Instead of impeding my view, I could clearly see the back of the van filled floor to ceiling with boxes of speakers. I could not see the hand I knew I was holding up in front of my face.

"I told you to close your eyes," the man said. "It makes you dizzy the first couple of times."

"W-what? W-w-what is—" That was all I could manage as my head spun faster.

The man quickly stepped closer and touched my shoulder to steady me.

"Now, just take it easy, friend," he said, lowering his voice to a hushed tone. "Stay calm. This is one of those special features I was telling you about."

"What's happening to me? What did you do?"

The man positioned himself directly in front of me and grabbed my other shoulder, applying firm pressure to each.

"I said calm down."

I felt the remote being yanked from my hand, and a second later, the music stopped. I pushed away from the man and realized I could see my hand against the man's chest. Attached to it was my arm, which I could also see. The man must have seen the confusion on my face transition to anger because he held his hands up in a defensive posture as I leveled my eyes at him.

"Just let me explain before you go all crazy, rich, white guy on me."

My anger subsided with this comment only because I'd never had anyone refer to me as 'crazy' or 'rich'. White guy, sure, but there were never any spicy adjectives to accompany it. I guess the 'crazy' thing was subjective, but 'rich' was not a word I'd use to describe my monetary status. The man gently moved me to the side of the open doors and stood where I had been moments ago.

"Let me show you something first, and then I'll explain . . . as best I can, at least."

He pointed the remote at the speakers and pressed a button. The song picked back up at the point it had been stopped, and for a moment, nothing happened. A second later, something did happen, something I was not prepared for. The man vanished. He was right there three feet away from me a second ago, and then he was just gone.

I felt nauseous as I was struck with the thought that I very well may be crazy. I tended to daydream, but having a full-blown hallucination was entirely new. I heard a car door open behind me and spun around to see the speaker man opening the door to my car from the inside before stepping out from the driver's side.

"Don't start to freak out," he said, holding his hands out. "I can explain everything. Those speakers right there, well, I told you they were very high-end."

"Yeah," I said, flustered, "you said they were every audiophile's wet dream because of their sound, not because of . . . of whatever the hell just happened."

"I did say that, and do they not sound like the best speakers you've ever heard?"

"I think that point is mute in light of—"

"Yes, the sound quality is just one of the premium features," the man spat, trying to keep me from launching into some 'crazy, rich, white guy' rant, "but that's not all these bad boys can do."

"Clearly not!"

I didn't realize I was shouting until the man raced over to me, glancing side to side to see if any of the gas-pumping patrons around us took notice. He got right up on me, pulled me close to his face, and spoke in a low, stern tone.

"Look, man, I'm trying to help *you* out here, so keep it down and stop making a scene!"

I, of course, wanted to launch into a rabid line of questioning on exactly how he was doing *me* a favor but became immediately distracted by how the man said it. Not his tone or cadence, but his accent, as in he suddenly had one. I was terrible at placing accents and had embarrassed myself enough times guessing origins when introduced to someone new with a foreign inflection. I wanted to say it sounded Middle Eastern, which I knew wasn't right, but I thought it sounded close. The man must have sensed my surprise and confusion because he loosened his grip on my shirt and softened his features.

"Listen, friend," he said in the same accent, letting me know I hadn't imagined it. "I'm sure you've realized by now that I'm not the typical lowlife conman trying to sell junk from the back of my van, and I've shown you these are not your typical speakers."

I was too stunned to speak, managing instead a few quiet gasps to communicate my feelings until my tongue and vocal cords could get back on the same page.

"No shit," I managed in a whisper.

"Yes, that's right," the man said. "No shit."

An uneasy, anxious moment passed between the man and me, with the both of us now wary of what the other may say or do. The man broke the tension by talking first.

"These speakers make the listener invisible and allow them to pass through solid objects. The sand you found inside, well, let's just say it didn't come from any beach you've heard of. I was serious when I said it made the speakers special. They wouldn't work at all without it."

I had no more outraged reactions left despite what the man just told me being extremely worthy of one. I'd seen it, though. I'd just witnessed the speaker do precisely what he said. I know there are high-level illusionists out there who can do some unbelievable things in their act, but this was something entirely different. I didn't know exactly what this man was trying to sell me, but it was legit.

"Okay, okay," I said, stepping back and running my hands through my hair several times, a nervous habit. "As hard as it is for me to say this, I believe you, but why would you be trying to sell something like that? Why are you so hell-bent on selling them to me?"

A moment of trepidation disrupted the man's calm expression so quickly you would miss it if you blinked. I wish I had blinked. As it did nothing to quell the uneasy feeling that gripped me.

"That is a hard question to answer," he said.

"Well, how about you try."

The man pulled a cigarette from the pack in his breast pocket, stuck it between his lips, and lit it with a lighter I didn't see him pull out. He drew deeply and paced a few steps while exhaling. His face was screwed into a thoughtful expression with a hint of worry hiding within the folds of his tan face.

"To put it as simply as I can," he said, pausing to take another drag. "I can't keep it anymore, and now I must give it to you."

"Hold on, that's putting it a little too simply, don't you think? How about you make it a little more complicated than that?"

"The sand within the speakers is old. Much older than you or I can fully comprehend. It's been passed from person to person throughout the years, dictating its path the entire way."

"Wait," I said, running my hand through my hair thrice. "Are you saying this sand wants me specifically to have it now and the same for you before me?"

The man lit up at this and smiled as silvery-white smoke leaked from his nostrils and the spaces between his fool's gold-colored teeth.

"Yes," he said excitedly. "Yes, exactly that! Now you see you must take the speakers, and I'll sell them cheap."

"Wait a second. First, I don't 'see'. Second, why would I have to pay you if the speakers, sand, or whatever *chose* me?"

The man took a long and final drag of his cigarette and flicked the butt off to the side. It hit the closest gas pump beside the nozzle and bounced off, dispersing glowing red remnants of the cherry across the ground. I wasn't as concerned by this as I had been earlier. I shook off the distraction and looked back to the man.

"It is a necessary formality of tradition in lieu of a sacrifice. Those were the old ways, so don't get worked up again. All I need is something in exchange for the sand. Then, the passing on is complete, and your time with the sand will begin."

I sighed, placed my hands on my hips, and started pacing the small area between the van and my car.

"I'm sure this is a stupid question, but I'm assuming I don't have a choice for some reason. Am I right?"

"You do have a choice," the man said hesitantly. "You can choose not to take the sand from me. I can't force you to do anything, but I assure you if that *is* your choice, there will be cataclysmic repercussions for the both of us."

"Yeah, I figured you'd say something like that."

The rest of my time spent with the man at the gas station was a blur that could have lasted five more minutes or a half hour. To be honest, the entire concept of time escaped my grasp for the duration of the exchange. The speakers, or more importantly, the sand, ended up costing me one dollar and thirty-seven cents, which was the total of loose change in the center console of my car.

I was tired of going round and round with the man that I finally took the things. If what I saw was all an elaborate and masterfully executed magic trick, then it cost me some time and pocket change. If I got them home and they didn't work, it was no big loss to just pitch them.

I put the speakers on the coffee table in my apartment and spent a little over an hour just staring at them from the couch. So many things bothered me, but I kept returning to the man's strange behavior as we made the transaction.

He was happy. That much was clear, but there was an underlying relief I picked up on. The man acted as though a weight had been lifted off him. His steps suddenly became lighter and livelier, and when he held out his hand to accept the change, I saw he was noticeably shaking. He closed his fingers around the dirty coins and then quickly walked to his van, thanking and assuring me the whole way. It was like he was shamefully fleeing from an awkward sexual encounter, promising he'd be sure to call.

There were no instructions with the speakers, but why would there be? I asked what the rest of the boxes marked 'speakers' in his van were, and he answered by pushing them over, revealing they were empty. The man said, "I didn't want to make you suspicious with just an empty van and the one set of speakers."

I was told they could be connected to any stereo or music-playing device despite the connectors at the end of the wires not looking like anything I'd seen before, but I was tired of asking questions that all seemed to have the same answer. The man said they were equipped with universal adaptors, so I took him at his word. I held the remote device in my right hand, stroking the smooth casing with my thumb. I'd examined it closely when I got home and found no seams on the entire thing, but I wasn't surprised. I didn't think the batteries dying would be something I'd have to worry about.

I looked closely at both speakers, turning each one repeatedly in my hand, looking for something I might have missed. The first thing I noticed was while I could feel the sand quietly shifting inside each speaker, not a single grain slipped through as it had back in the van. Any space I'd observed between the edge of the speaker and the box was now nonexistent, as if they'd sealed on their own somewhere between the gas station and my apartment.

I studied every inch of both speakers, searching for any indication of normality until my eyes were too fatigued to focus. I dug through the junk drawer in my kitchen until I found a small microfiber cloth for cleaning lenses and other delicate surfaces. I carefully ran the fabric over the speakers, meticulously removing any trace of dust, hoping to uncover the imperfection I was searching for, but there was nothing.

I turned one of the speakers over and lightly tugged on the wires protruding from the back to see if I could gain entry that way, but they stuck firm with no give. I yanked harder, but they held fast, giving a phantom sensation they were pulling back. There was something oddly organic about them, like they had grown out of the speaker rather than having been attached by the manufacturer. Then, I finally found something.

It was faint, and I would have never discovered it if the light hadn't reflected off the area just right. On the back of one of the speakers, beneath the wires, was a tiny symbol etched into the wood. It was either worn away from age or purposely made to be nearly undetectable, but it was there. Barely. I checked the other speaker in the same spot under a lamp, trying to find the right angle to make the mark appear. It suddenly became visible, like I'd been staring at one of those 'magic eye' pictures for hours before it finally clicked.

The best I could tell, they looked like symbols of some kind, but not any I'd ever seen. They were reminiscent of the ankhs that marked the tombs of Egyptian pharaohs, but not quite the same. Additional lines to the symbol set them apart from the closest thing they resembled to me. Most electronics are made in foreign countries, but this looked beyond foreign. These symbols looked ancient.

From my couch, I performed a short image search on my phone for ancient Egyptian symbols, hieroglyphs, and even some occult-related sigils. Still, I couldn't find anything similar, and my head already ached from straining my eyes, looking back and forth between the screen and the essentially invisible imprint on the speakers. I tossed my phone on the cushion next to me, but not before noting the time was 10:37 p.m. I'd been examining my spontaneous purchase for over three hours, looking for a reason not to believe they actually did what the man said they did when I could've found out immediately by just trying them out.

I grabbed my phone and placed it on the coffee table between the two speakers. The man showed me how the 'universal adapters' at the end of the wires fit together and folded back to become one single ¾ inch input that fits the output of my phone. I didn't have a component stereo, but the man assured me if I got one, it would be easy to figure out how to affix the speaker wire to whatever outputs the receiver had. I mainly used my phone to listen to music through a shitty, blown-out, blue tooth speaker or the auxiliary input in my car.

I took the ends of the wire from each speaker, repeated the steps I'd seen the man carry out, and slowly inserted it into the output jack of my phone until it clicked into place. I put the phone back down on the table between the speakers, pretending I was trying to decide what to listen to, but I was only stalling.

I was more nervous the speakers would work than not, and my stomach twisted in and over itself, tangling with my small intestine, enhancing impending doom I hadn't been able to shake since I'd left the gas station.

"Fuck it," I said out loud, running my hands through my hair five or six times.

I picked up the phone from the table and began scrolling through my saved music. I thumbed down the list, back up, down the bottom again, and back up again before I realized I was only stalling again. My hand was shaking, and I gripped my phone harder to avoid the tremors before bringing my thumb down on the screen. The album I'd selected at random cast a pale purple-tinted illumination across my face, and I looked down to see *Masters of Reality, Black Sabbath.*

The letters were stylized and twisted in a way I always thought looked like psychedelic turned Goth. The presentation mocked the happy, sunshine, flowery feel of other bands at the time, coopting the sentiment by making a dark mockery of the shiny veneer in which their contemporaries were shellacked. This wasn't necessarily the record I would have consciously chosen for the test run I was about to take, but it felt strangely apropos for the experience.

As much as I wanted to allow myself to be convinced I needed to choose another album, I knew I would have the same feeling regardless of what I decided. I placed my phone back on the table between the speakers, pointed the smooth, cool, stone-like remote in its direction, and gently brought my thumb down on one of the buttons.

A warm hiss began to leak from the speakers low at first, then quickly swelled in volume as the album launched into the evil-sounding reverb-drenched cough that gave me goosebumps as a kid every time I heard it. The opening lick to the song *Sweet Leaf* followed on the heels of the cough's decay, and my body began to tingle like ants beneath my skin were burrowing their way out through my follicles.

I didn't remember closing my eyes, but I must have because I remember opening them. The disorienting tingle at the gas station was overwhelming this time, so I thought I'd vibrate to pieces. Every part of my body seemed to fall asleep at once, sending the sensation of pins and needles through me like I'd been locked in an iron maiden.

As the sensation subsided, my eyelids fluttered open, but I noticed no apparent difference in my surroundings until I lifted my hand before my face. I could feel I was still holding the remote and squeezing it tight to reassure myself, but there was nothing in the space before me where I should have been seeing my fingers clutching the odd object. I lifted my other hand, waving it about like I was trying to hail a cab during rush hour, and it was transparent as well.

I no longer required convincing of the speaker's ability, but it was time for the second phase of my test run. I stood, finding it more difficult than it should have been. A residual tingle lingered in my legs, and my head spun like I'd just stepped off the Tilt-A-Whirl. The top half of my body felt like it was not proportionally balanced with my lower half, and I overcorrected the weight adjustment, causing me to lose my balance. I pitched forward, holding invisible hands in time to catch myself on the coffee table.

I paused, holding onto the table's edge, getting used to feeling myself touch things without seeing them. A few seconds later, the spinning in my head slowed, then stopped, and I pushed up from the table, standing on considerably less shaky legs.

I turned my head from one side to the other, slowly scanning the living room, and as far as I could tell, everything appeared as it should, with just one slight difference. Darkness. The entire area around me was noticeably darker, as if I were wearing sunglasses inside. The second difference took longer to realize, but it became apparent as I cautiously moved away from the couch to explore further. It was the song.

I could still hear it, which should have been a given since I stood next to the speakers, but there was a marked difference now. The tremendous warmth and clarity the speakers imbued to music, lucky enough to be pumped through their superior craftsmanship, was no more.

The fidelity had been wiped completely, compressing it to make it sound like I was listening to it underwater. The strangest thing was I heard it playing at the same volume regardless of my proximity to the speakers like a garbled, unlistenable version of the song had been implanted in the back left portion of my brain.

I first noticed as I turned the corner into the hallway, strolling, unsure of what I was doing. I thought maybe the speakers were following me, and I'd turn around to find them levitating just over my shoulder. Of course, that wasn't the case, but I stopped and returned to the living room to be sure. I put my ear right against one of the speakers and then backed up to the far wall across the room. The volume in my head didn't waiver a single decibel in either direction.

I began taking a litany of notes in my head of what I was experiencing to compare the next time I tried the speakers. I wanted to keep track in case the experience varied based on location or variables between inside versus outside, temperature, and anything else I could think of to ensure I remembered.

I started back down the hall with the low-fi version of *Sweet Leaf* playing in my head and stopped in front of the closed bathroom door. It was time to test what these speakers supposedly could do in the second half. I stepped back from the door, putting about two and a half feet between it and myself. Then, I took a solid and confident step forward, after which I hit the door face-first. The impact was hard enough to rattle it against the frame, sending white streaks of light back and forth across my vision.

"Fuck!"

I rubbed the bump with my invisible hand and realized I could hear my voice just fine, loud and clear. It remained unaffected by whatever was hampering my ability to listen to sounds happening around me.

I still heard Ozzy squealing his way through *Sweet Leaf* in the far back corner of my head and could tell the song was at the halfway point despite the compromised clarity. I forgot I was still holding the remote until I felt an ache in my fingers from squeezing it so hard. Why hadn't I been able to pass through the door? The speakers worked so far in making me invisible, but why was I being denied the second half of the ride?

My blood pressure rose as frustration worked up my spine to close off my throat, but I curbed the reflex before its grip grew firm. Getting angry again wasn't going to help me walk through the door. I figured there had to be something I wasn't doing right; I was missing something. I stared at the door and thought about what it would be like to pass through a solid object, then narrowed my focus to what it would be like to pass through a door, more specifically, that door.

That was when I saw the door change.

It was subtle, but enough to know what I saw wasn't a trick of the light or a product of fatigued vision. The door was in front of me as it had been, but now I could see spaces between the energy that made it up. It was soft and malleable, like living quicksand swirling in on itself repeatedly.

I tuned everything out except the last remaining measures of *Sweet Leaf* chugging from the base of my skull. I stepped forward and walked through the door I had run face-first into a minute earlier. The song's final note sounded like stepping into the bathroom, but everything changed as it decayed.

The bathroom looked like it always had in that gone was the gritty, noir-esque coated reality I'd seen in the living room and hallway. The light was on, and I turned toward the mirror to see my reflection. I held my hands before me and could no longer see through them. I was visible again.

I hadn't pushed any buttons on the remote, which I could also see was still clutched tightly in my fist. It took me several panicky seconds later to realize what had changed. The song was no longer playing in my head, and instead of being followed by the laser-like intro of *After Forever*, as I had anticipated, there was nothing. Silence.

I stepped to the sink to splash water on my face but was stopped short by something my shirt was caught on. I reached back and turned around to pull it from the snare and immediately felt sick. As much as my body wanted to expel the contents of my stomach over what I saw, I was too shocked to puke.

My shirt wasn't caught *on* something, but rather *in* something. An inch and a half of my shirttail was stuck in the door. Not stuck between the door and the frame but within the door itself right at the center where I'd passed through. I tugged, but it held firm, and I was afraid to yank it any harder.

After my first attempt walking through a solid object, I discovered much about the speakers. Technically, I didn't learn anything new about the speakers themselves, but more about the idiosyncrasies that went along with how they worked. I started calling these 'the rules.' I spent the rest of that first night testing the odd ability the speakers granted. I documented my findings in a pocket-sized, spiral notebook I'd gotten for free from the new *Lucky Sack* grocery store two blocks from my apartment.

I visited the store during its grand opening and was given a plastic bag filled with swag like a notepad, a pencil, a pen, a Frisbee, a sweatband, and a keychain. All the items were emblazoned with a four-leaf clover marked in the center with the letters 'LS' in the store's custom font.

It took me more than a few minutes to come down from the freak out I experienced when my shirt got stuck in the door, or more accurately, fused with the door itself. I'd yanked the shirt several times, accomplishing nothing but stretching out the material, so I slipped out of the shirt to look closer at the attached area. The shirt seemed to be a part of the door now, and I retrieved a pair of scissors for facial hair trimming from the drawer beneath the bathroom sink.

I cut the shirt as close to the door as possible but left a small amount of frayed material sprouting out like a patch of mold on a tree. I went to the kitchen and rummaged through drawers until I found a box cutter, used my fingernail to loosen the single screw holding the device's handle together, and removed the razor blade from inside. I took the blade back to the bathroom and carefully used it to scrape away loose threads until the material was flush with the door.

The small piece of my shirt had undoubtedly become part of the door. I ran my fingers over the area back and forth, then up and down, and felt no difference in texture between it and the rest of the wood. I needed to learn the rules of how this whole thing worked, and since there wasn't an instruction book, I'd have to figure them out on my own through good ol' trial and error.

The first thing I wrote in the *Lucky Sack* notebook was a list of everything that happened during the first time. I listed everything from the speaker's location to the fabric, size, and shirt's color. I went down the list and put a star next to variables I thought might be more likely to dictate certain aspects of the experience and decided to test them one by one.

The duration of any song played through the speakers clearly dictated how long I remained invisible. I also found only one song would play at a time, no matter how many I cued up in a row. There was no way to make the album continue to the next track or even repeat.

What troubled me most was what happened to my shirt, so I tried to recreate the experience. I took my shirt off while the song played and planned to plunge it through the coffee table at the end but found it didn't work that way. As soon as I removed the article of clothing, it wasn't invisible anymore, and no matter how hard I concentrated, I couldn't move the shirt through a solid object unless it was physically on my person.

I suspended all disbelief by this point and noted my findings in the *Lucky Sack* notebook. This was happening, and I accepted it, but I needed to know everything about whatever the speakers did to me. Besides, I was starting to have some fun. I'd walked through all the walls in my apartment from one side to the other and back.

I didn't attempt to walk through the walls I shared with my neighbors on either side because I wanted to find out all I could within a controlled environment before venturing out. I put my hand through the refrigerator door and discovered a contradiction to what happened when I tried to push my shirt through the coffee table.

Without thinking, I wrapped my fingers around a cold bottle of light beer and pulled it through the door. I couldn't see the bottle but knew I was holding it. I could feel condensation dampen my fingers as the bottle began to sweat from the temperature change, and my hand was quite familiar with the weight and heft of twelve fluid ounces in a brown glass bottle.

I didn't need to see the bottle to twist off the cap, so I did. I flung it to the floor and became visible as it bounced off a cabinet, skidded across the badly stained linoleum, and disappeared under the stove. I brought the bottle to my lips, tilted my head back, and took in three-quarters of the bottle's contents.

The rapid beer intake on an empty stomach gave me an unexpected head rush, but then I realized the song I was listening to had ended, and with it did the speakers' effect. I was listening to *Enter the Void* now. It's the same album, different songs. Seeing the bottle in my hand and the sensation of becoming visible was startling. I stumbled forward and caught the counter's edge but dropped the bottle, which shattered at my feet.

I stood still, stared down at the bits of broken glass mixed with beer and foam, and lost track of time. I watched the suds fizzle into small puddles of flat beer that crept slowly toward the stove, absorbing the glass it came and with a potpourri of crumbs and loose grime. I snapped out of it and stepped over the puddle, hoping it would disappear beneath the stove like the cap had.

I didn't know why I could pull the bottle through the refrigerator door but couldn't push my shirt through the coffee table, and I didn't like it. I was trying to figure out the rules of how these things worked, and the fact I'd already found a contradiction after only a few tests unsettled me.

Back in the living room, I took the remote from my pocket and pressed a button to repeat the song. I didn't have to be standing in front of the speakers for them to work on me anymore. I guess they knew they belonged to me now. *Into the Void* kicked off again, and I closed my eyes, waiting for the strange sensation to pass.

I returned to the kitchen and stopped when I saw the glassy puddle. It had gotten closer to creeping under the stove but still had a ways to go and was clearly losing steam. I debated whether I should clean it or keep stepping over it while nodding to the distorted monotone beat of the song playing in my head.

A strange noise cut through the dulled din in my head, and I thought it sounded like the doorbell. It *was* the doorbell. I didn't realize I was doing it until it was happening, but I found myself at the front door opening it up.

A woman was standing there who I didn't recognize. She had short brown hair down to her chin that framed her lightly tanned face, but her eyes were far too striking not to be the first thing anybody noticed about her. They were a light shade of green with an emerald quality I'd never seen before. They stood out despite the dull, dark wash I experienced while invisible.

I couldn't help but stare; it seemed like she was staring right back. She *was* staring right back. The woman took off a backpack slung over her shoulder and threw it past me into the apartment.

"Oh man, you are so fucked," she said. "Oh, and I can see you, by the way."

I stood still, unsure how to answer or what to say if I did.

"Are you gonna' invite me in?" The woman seethed with confidence and attitude. "Actually, let me put it this way. Remember how I said you were fucked? I'm the only one who can help you un-fuck yourself, but you gotta let me in first."

I stepped to the side, and she breezed past me into the apartment. I shut the door, and the song ended.

The woman's name was Gwen. It was Guinevere because her parents were really into knights, castles, and Renaissance fairs before she was born. Now, they were into stock portfolios and retirement, and she was into going by Gwen.

She'd pulled a chair out from the kitchen and put it on the other side of the coffee table across from where I had been sitting on the couch. We were both holding cold bottles of light beer I retrieved from the refrigerator the old-fashioned way, opening and closing the door. Gwen took a drink from her beer, prompting me to as well, and I noticed she was almost finished while I'd hardly taken my first sip.

"So," she started, "how long have you had them?"

I didn't have to ask. I knew she was referring to the speakers.

"Not long. Maybe around eight or nine hours."

"Damn!" Gwen slapped her knee. "I told him I could find you in five."

"Told who?"

"Never mind." Gwen put the bottle to her lips and tilted her head back, taking the remainder of her beer down her throat. "Why would you— Well, we'll cover that later. What have you already figured out?"

"Figured out? Cover what later?"

"Look," Gwen put the empty bottle on the table harder than necessary, but it caught my attention. "This would go a lot faster if you stopped answering my questions with questions."

"I'm sorry," I said, sitting up straighter and taking a long drink from my beer. "I'm just—"

"Overwhelmed, yeah, I get it," she said. "I'll try to be more delicate if that helps, but you only have a finite amount of time in which I can help. After that, it won't matter anymore, so it's totally up to you."

"Won't matter? I mean . . . okay. They make me invisible, the speakers."

"Of course, you know that. I'm sure he used it as a major selling point."

Gwen went to bring the bottle to her lips but remembered it was empty and just looked down at it instead.

"Can I get you another beer? There's plenty in the fridge."

"I'll get it," she said, jumping to her feet.

Gwen was more than halfway to the kitchen before I could protest, and a moment later, she was back in her chair with two long-neck bottles dangling from the fingers of her left hand. A third bottle was clutched tight in her right with the cap already off. Gwen set one of the beers on the table in front of me and placed the third on the table in front of her.

"I'm a fast drinker," she said, noticing my confused look. "I'm just saving myself another trip. What else have you found out?"

"Do you know who this guy w—" I stopped myself, realizing I was asking another question. "Sorry. I guess they allow me to pass through walls and other solid objects. I haven't tried on too many different things."

Over the next half hour, I told Gwen everything I'd learned about the speakers through unscientific self-testing. I mostly talked to her, with Gwen offering very little response, but she was noticeably intently listening to every word I said. I could see the gears turning in her brain, processing each detail of my story as I told it.

I recounted my experience slightly out of order, saving my primary question and concern for last. When I told her about pulling the beer through the fridge door but being unable to push my shirt through the table, I expected more of a reaction. Instead, I got a lot of nodding and a few well-placed, random 'hmm' sounds with no further explanation.

When I told her about the piece of my shirttail fusing with the bathroom door, Gwen reacted as if I'd thrown a bucket of ice water on her. She shot up haphazardly, setting her third beer, which she'd already emptied half of, on the edge of the coffee table.

I reached to pull the bottle further away from the edge, but Gwen was already emphatically calling for me to show her down the hall. When I made it to her, she was already in the bathroom. I found her crouching on the tile floor, running her fingers back and forth over the spot in question. Gwen was familiar with this phenomenon and could see the area without my help.

"You're lucky," she said, still studying the area without looking at me. "If I'd have taken much longer to find you, it would probably have been too late."

"Too late?"

I realized I was asking another question, but it was one of genuine concern since Gwen's demeanor was so severe. She'd found an errant black thread I must have missed with the razorblade, held it between her thumb and forefinger and yanked hard to pull it from the door like she was pulling a single hair out by the root. She looked from the thread in her hand to the door and back again before speaking.

"If the song ended a second sooner, you would've been slicing a piece of your back off to get free, and that never works as well as you think."

I suppressed my urge to ask another question, emitting an audible gulp instead. Gwen stood up and pointed to the area on the door where my shirt had been attached.

"This spot right here," she started, "well, that's not a piece of your shirt anymore. Same with the area on the door it was sticking out from, it's something different now."

"Different, how?"

I didn't care about asking questions anymore since I felt I'd fully explained myself. The absurdity of what my reality had become over the last several hours started sinking in, and I suddenly found myself a pussy hair away from a full-blown panic attack.

"Come on," she said, pushing me out of the bathroom. "I need the rest of that beer, and you must catch up."

Gwen did the majority of the talking for the next hour over the rest of the beers I had left. She explained that I was only partially correct when I became what I called invisible. It wasn't like in the movies where a cape draped across your head causes you to appear transparent to who you're trying to elude. The light wasn't somehow being bent around me to confuse the naked eye into not seeing me either. According to Gwen, what happened to me was related to vibration and space.

When the speakers played, every part of my being vibrated so intensely that the molecules pushed away to increase the space between them. She told me this was how I could envision the bathroom door before walking through it the first time. The space created wasn't enough to cause a complete dispersal of my energy, but it was enough to make me appear invisible to people around me, including myself. I didn't understand, but I accepted it, knowing even a lengthy explanation would confuse me further.

While the vibration opened the space between my molecules, the same vibration allowed me to touch or hold objects. Gwen said specific actions, like picking something up, are so natural and ingrained in our brain the vibration changes when said action is executed.

To attach the thing to a hand whose particles aren't as close together as they used to be, they alter the vibrations to pull the object into where you perceive your hand is. Gwen said to think of it in the same way magnets attract metal, only these magnets attract whatever I'm reaching to pick up. My hand is far too spread out to grab anything, but the particles fool my brain into thinking I can feel and control my hand.

In short, every time I used the speakers, my body was blown apart into a billion pieces that all worked together to fool me into feeling the sensation of my body as I knew it instead of the formless floating cloud of vibrating particles that I was.

When I asked about my clothes, Gwen told me anything I wear when the speakers play becomes subject to the same thing. My particles were vibrating so violently they couldn't help but disrupt what was hugged up against them, or in other words, my clothes. She said my particles were holding the particles of my clothing hostage. My shirt became visible when I removed it because all my particles let go instantly, allowing it to be whole again.

She was giving me the bare-boned layman version of what was happening, and while I know I wouldn't understand if she laid it all out in technical terms, it would've been fun to try.

"So, what's the deal with the shirt then?" I asked, pacing the living room while Gwen stayed seated, drinking her fifth beer. "The part that got stuck in the door, or whatever. You said it was different now. What was that?"

"That was really lucky for you."

"How so?" It was my turn to drain more than half my beer in one sip.

"The area of the door where your shirt was stuck is different now because it's become intertwined with the door. It's not just sharing the space like they're stacked up on each other; the particles from the shirt and door have fused together, becoming something that's neither one nor the other now."

I finished my beer and went to the kitchen for another. Only two were left, and as I reached for one, Gwen called for me to bring her one too.

"Why did that happen? To the shirt, I mean. Why didn't it come through with the rest?"

I shut the refrigerator door with my hip and twisted the silver caps off both bottles. Gwen waited to answer until I'd returned to the room and handed her the beer.

"Because the song stopped," she said. "Think about it like a form of musical chairs except when the music stops in this game, you don't want to be passing through anything solid. Otherwise, what happened to your shirt happens to you."

It was close to four in the morning when I'd exhausted all my questions for Gwen, or at least the ones I could think of. All the beer was gone, and I ran to the convenience store for another twelve-pack, then swung through the all-night drive-thru of *Burger Perjure* for a very late dinner. *Burger Perjure* was a courtroom-themed burger joint with the slogan *A Burger so Good, You'll Lie Under Oath.*

The front-of-house employees all wore judge's robes with a plastic nametag pinned to their chest while the 'cooks', if you want to call them that, wore what looked like hospital scrubs with a bailiff uniform printed on them. As corny as the themed restaurant was, they made some damn good burgers, all it took for patrons to go along with the silliness or at least look past it.

When I returned to the apartment, Gwen sat on the couch where I'd been most of the evening. She was leaning back, staring at the speakers with the remote in her left hand. She was absently running her thumb up and down the side of the smooth stone object.

According to her, the remote was not integral to making the speakers work but more of an aftermarket addition. You could use it to start any device; turning it on manually was still an option. Its only other purpose was to prematurely stop the music. Apparently, it would work no matter how far away you were from the source. When I asked why there were four buttons for only one function, Gwen brushed it off, saying they were for aesthetics.

We sat and ate silently at the coffee table with the speakers between us. The only sound was the occasional burp following a sip of beer or unintentional lip-smacking from myself as I voraciously

devoured my *Supreme Court Justice Burger.* A hulking two beef patties stacked high with everything else you can think of, hence *supreme.*

Gwen didn't eat meat, so I got her a vegetarian *Alford Burger.* The restaurant claimed after trying one, you'd have to confess to being guilty of eating meat no matter how innocent you knew you were. She finished her beer before I'd taken my second sip, being too focused on eating. I didn't realize how hungry I was until I sat down and unwrapped my burger. I'd been so consumed with the speakers and this strange woman showing up I'd forgotten to eat.

I finally paused between bites and looked at the burger in my hand. I thought about how Gwen explained why I could pull the bottle of beer through the refrigerator door but couldn't push the shirt through the table. She said the simple explanation was because of size and surface area. There was too much shirt for my particles to reach out and pull them apart. Gwen said it would have passed right through if I'd tried something I could fit in my hand, like the beer bottle or my wallet.

The sound of Gwen popping open another beer snapped me from my meat daze, and my stomach retook control, forcing me to continue stuffing the burger into my mouth. Three larger-than-recommended bites later, the burger was gone, a greasy, wadded wrapper the only evidence of its existence. I started on my fries while Gwen was still only a couple bites deep into her burger.

"So," I finally said, attempting to slow my gorge, "you mentioned earlier about not having much time. Why does that matter? How much time *do* I have, and what happens if I run out?"

Gwen chewed slowly and thoughtfully like a child trying to stall to think of the best answer to give a parent questioning their behavior. I used the opportunity to shove five fries into my mouth, followed by a long swig of beer gone warm.

"It's tough to gauge the amount of time," she said after swallowing. "It's always different, but I know one thing for sure. If I'm here, it means you don't have long."

I chewed slowly and took in her statement, waiting for the rest of an answer that didn't come.

"Well, what happens? What happens when this undetermined amount of time expires?"

"Honestly," she said, placing the remainder of her burger still wrapped in wax paper on the coffee table, "telling you now would not be productive. I promise I'll tell you when it's close, but it might be too late. If you trust me and let me help, there's a good chance you won't even get to that point."

A slew of questions flooded from my brain, threatening to rapid-fire out of my mouth, but were stopped short behind the 'don't ask questions' wall I had left up from our earlier conversation. Gwen had to have known what was going on in my mind because the look on her face let me know my inquiries would not, or *could* not be answered at this time.

As much as I wanted to launch my rapid-fire follow-up questions, I changed the subject.

"So," I started taking a bite of burger and finishing the thought with my mouthful, "do you know the guy who sold these to me? Do you work for him or something? He didn't even tell me his name."

Gwen had stuffed a handful of fries into her mouth and held a hand up, signifying the answer would come once she'd swallowed, which it did.

"Work for him? No, I do not, and you're better off not knowing his name."

"Why, is he dangerous or something? Do I need to worry about this guy?"

Gwen chewed the last of her fries while shaking her head until enough potato slid down her throat to allow her tongue the room to maneuver effectively.

"No," she said flatly, swallowing what little was left tucked in her cheeks. "I need to worry about him. You need to—"

"I know, I know, stop asking questions. Given the situation, I hope you understand that's hard to do now. I bought speakers out of a van that causes temporal displacement, and a strange woman shows up at my apartment claiming to know all about it but won't tell me."

I instantly regretted letting my frustration show and adjusted my body language on the fly to seem more apathetic than aggressive. I shrugged, hoping it came off casually, put the beer to my lips, and threw my head back to empty the bottle. I put it down and saw Gwen had leaned in like she was going to say something but only stared instead.

A silver chain fell from the front of her shirt with a small charm dangling from it. I tried to make out the design from across the table, but Gwen stuffed it down her shirt when she noticed it. I brought my eyes back up to meet hers.

"Temporal displacement has to do with traveling through time and is largely known to be unproven," she said, breaking the tension I'd wedged between us through my outburst. "You are being spread out to the point where you can travel through solid mass but not through time. Also, I'm sure I don't have to tell you're not in a sci-fi movie trope either."

Now, it was my turn to be silent for a few seconds. I felt like I was being talked to like a petulant child, and while I may have been acting like one on some level, I still didn't appreciate her tone. I would have to lighten up and go with it because Gwen held all the cards tightly to her chest. She had me over a barrel simply by having the information I wanted but, in her opinion, didn't *need it*.

"You're right," I said, significantly softening my tone. "The lack of sleep is starting to catch up with me. Could I grab a quick nap before we get back into it? I think it would do wonders to clear my head some."

She was already shaking her head before I finished my sentence.

"Sleep is *not* what you need right now, trust me."

I liked how Gwen said 'trust me' as if I had a choice.

"Okay, okay," I answered, immediately fighting the urge to *want* to know why. "So, if sleeping is out, what's the next step?"

I realized I asked a question while trying not to ask a different question, but I felt this one was innocuous. I wasn't asking for instructions, not reasons and explanations."

"Follow me," Gwen said, bounding from the couch toward the hall, "and grab the speakers."

I grabbed a speaker under each arm, tucked my phone into my back pocket, and walked to the end of the hall, where I found Gwen in my bedroom. She stood at the wall, running her hands over the space before her.

"Here," Gwen said.

She turned around, saw me standing at the door, and nodded as she continued to scan the room. Her eyes landed on the desk against the opposite wall, and she cleared the distance in two long, quick strides. She grabbed something from the desktop and was back at the wall half a second later. I realized she'd taken a marker as I watched her use it to draw a large X on the wall before her.

"Bring in the speakers and set them up on the desk."

She was still staring at the X as I went to the desk, knocking books and papers to the floor with my elbow to make room. I'd left the wires in the same configuration, plugged it into my phone, and awaited further instructions. Gwen narrowed her eyes at the wall and gave a slight and subtle nod before turning her attention to me. She crossed to the desk before she spoke.

"Now I can tell you," she started. "Now I can tell you what's happening to you and what you need to do to stop it." Gwen paused as if she'd said something that elicited a response and was clearly waiting for it.

'Thank you?" I replied with a shrug, not wanting to ask a question and further delay the release of information.

Gwen rolled her eyes and walked past me, looking down at the speakers and straightening them on the desk while knocking more items to the floor. Among them was a Coor's koozie I kept pens in and a pad of post-its I'd made into a naughty flipbook of a penis going from flaccid to fully erect, then shooting gooey jizzum spurts across the page upon reaching full engorgement. I mentally noted where it landed to retrieve it once it was over. I planned on adding further detail and didn't want to start entirely from scratch.

Satisfied with her arrangement of the speakers, Gwen turned to face me, leaned back against the desk, and folded her arms across her chest. She looked me up and down before her eyes landed on my face, which she studied intently for several seconds. She leaned in toward me, and for a second, I thought a Cinemax-after-dark-type situation was about to happen.

At that moment, I imagined her grabbing the back of my head and pulling my face into hers for a lust-driven, sloppy kiss, during which we would clumsily stumble across the room to my bed, shedding clothing along the way. I suddenly regretted not changing my sheets for over a month and hoped Gwen wouldn't notice in the heat of passion.

My mind raced, remembering if I had any condoms left on my nightstand. Not that I used them so much that I couldn't keep track of my inventory, but quite the opposite. It had been several months since my last sexual encounter, and I honestly couldn't remember if I'd even used a condom then. Maybe she wouldn't notice or be one of those girls who hated condoms, or she—

"It started," said Gwen in a tone that told me she was *not* thinking what I was thinking. "It's already happening."

"It is?" I said, feeling my face turn red, embarrassed by my assumption. "I mean, what is?"

"The curse," she said with nonchalance, like talking about a curse was something she brought up in daily conversation. "The man who sold you the speakers was cursed when he received them, but now that he's gotten you to buy them, he's successfully passed the curse on to you."

I was shocked not because of how ridiculous being told I was cursed was but because of how utterly plausible and obvious it sounded. I realized everything that happened to me since pulling up to get gas that afternoon ultimately lent itself to an old movie trope involving passing a cursed object from one person to the next, usually involving some trickery.

I was reminded of a very old Abbott and Costello bit in which the duo meets a mummy and is terrified of receiving its horrid curse. I felt just as foolish as the classic comedy team, but in the way I was being laughed at and not with. My mind was reeled with questions now, and there was no way to keep them from spilling out anymore.

"That's how it works?" I finally managed. "I just take speakers, and suddenly I'm wham, bam, thank you ma'am cursed? Don't you have to cast a spell to curse someone, stroke their face, and say *thinner* or something else?"

Gwen seemed unaffected by my questions and started pacing in front of my desk, kicking at the books, papers, and other items my floor was littered with. She shook her head and smiled, but not a comforting smile. This was the kind of smile that said, *you poor bastard.*

"This isn't the movies." The words fell from her mouth like hunks of granite, each shaking the ground slightly more than the one before it. "Also, you didn't *take* the speakers. You bought them. That's why you're cursed."

"Bought them? I gave the guy change from the console of my car for them. I don't even think it was even a whole dollar!"

"Doesn't matter," said Gwen, still pacing, still kicking at the junk on my floor. "If someone who is cursed manages to sell the item responsible for cursing them, the curse is passed to the one who paid for it."

"But isn't there some sort of 'buyer beware' clause that says he has to disclose the curse associated with the item being sold? Wouldn't he have to give me some choice, or ultimatum, at least have me fill out a questionnaire or something?"

"I told you this isn't the movies," scoffed Gwen, "and you were given a choice of whether to buy the speakers or not, and you *chose* to buy them."

"Well, I wouldn't have chosen to buy them if I had been told the speakers included a curse at no extra charge!"

"Nobody would," continued Gwen, her inflection indicating she was becoming annoyed with my questions. "I know it doesn't sound fair, but that's how it works."

"So what then?" Now, it was my turn to sound annoyed. "Are you here to help me sell my curse to some other schlub, or will you buy it yourself?"

Gwen didn't answer right away, attempting to stall my frustration, which worked, leaving me feeling foolish for my outburst. I'd expected her to surpass my intensity, or at least match it, setting the bar to beat with my next round of heated questioning. I'd sprinted off a cliff, expecting to run across the air, only to lose my momentum and plummet to the ground.

"Right now," she started. "Right now, at this very moment, you are literally falling apart. Microscopic particles are detaching themselves from the energy that has until now kept them in place. It's too subtle to notice, but it won't stay that way long."

Goosebumps exploded from the flesh on my arms as a chill wrapped and slithered up my spine to the back of my neck, igniting the gooseflesh residing there. She said I couldn't feel it, but the phantom sensation of tiny pieces of myself floating away crawled across random parts of my body. I absently scratched at my forearms and shoulders.

Something suddenly changed in me, and the anger and anxiety fell away. I felt calm, composed, and ready to stop being argumentative. As far as I knew, I could be minutes from separating into microscopic particles. I'd accepted it would happen whether it was minutes, hours, days, or even seconds. If Gwen was the only one who could help me stop that from happening, I needed to start listening.

"I'm sorry," I said, the edge gone from my voice. "I'm kind of freaked out, but I shouldn't have snapped at you. I know you're here to help me, so I'll shut up and let you help. Now, what do I need to do?"

The hardness of Gwen's expression dulled and then softened, and her brow returned to its usual arch rising from the downward slant. I'm unsure if she was more taken aback by the change in my attitude or the apology, but I could tell she hadn't expected either.

"It's fine, don't worry about it," she said quickly, blowing past having to further acknowledge the change. "Let's do this to get out of each other's hair."

I nodded, and Gwen turned back around to the speakers. She plugged the strangely adaptable wires back into my phone, picked it up, and started to thumb through my music library. I didn't remember giving her the code to unlock my phone, but I figured she must have seen me punch it in.

"You like Sabbath," Gwen said, still scrolling, "like, a lot."

"I guess you could say that."

Gwen set the phone on the desk, removed the remote from her pocket, and pointed at the 'X' drawn on the wall with her other hand. I didn't remember giving Gwen the remote or seeing her put it in her pocket, but it was in her hand now, so she must have. I crossed to the marked area on the wall semi-sideways, watching Gwen as I went, and she followed me over a second later.

"Okay," she started after taking a deep breath, "here's how it's gonna' go. I'll start the music, and once you go 'poof', you need to pass through the wall right where I've marked, but take it slow. Don't just throw yourself through."

I looked from Gwen to the 'X' and back, and she told me the answer to the question I hadn't yet asked.

"I know there's not another room on the other side for you to walk through, but it's unnecessary for what we're doing."

I stood in silence, waiting for her to continue.

"It's hard to explain, but what you'll be stepping into is like a tunnel. Flashing lights will swirl around you so quickly it creates an illusion of what equates to a tunnel."

"But I won't actually be in a tunnel?"

"No."

"Then where will I be?"

"It doesn't matter," she snapped. "The tunnel will reverse your energy, keeping any more of you from breaking away while attracting particles you've already lost back. In a sense, it's reversing the curse and making you whole again."

"That's great," I said, genuinely believing it was. "That's great, but where do I come out? How do I get back here?"

"You just walk." She was turning the remote over and over in her hand. "You take two or maybe three steps and come out right here."

Gwen pointed back at the 'X'.

"I come out the same way I went in? So, do I need to take two steps, turn around, and take two more steps to come back out?"

"No. You'll just walk through, take a couple steps, and come out back here. No turning around necessary."

"What happens then?"

"What do you mean what happens? You're un-cursed."

"I get that," I said, looking at the 'X' on the wall, "but what happens to the speakers? What happens to you? Do I come back out, and they're gone, and so are you? Is there like an exit interview, or do we have to burn the ceremonious burn speakers and scatter the sand?"

A mix of impatience and anger flashed across Gwen's face so briefly I would've missed it had I blinked. A toothy smile followed quickly on the heels of it, more than likely meant to disarm me, which it did.

"No, nothing like that," she said lightly, "but one step at a time. I could stand here and explain the rest to you, but there may not be enough of you left to even remember what I'd just told you."

The same shiver rocked through my body, and I could feel the microscopic pieces of me breaking off and floating away at that moment, unnerving me. I started nodding my head immediately.

"You're right. Okay, let's do this."

"Good," she said, sounding slightly too eager, but I was probably misinterpreting her tone. "I'm going to hit the music. After you feel the change, step forward slowly. Don't rush, okay. Take it nice and slow."

I faced the 'X' on the wall and nodded. The last twelve hours of my life had been a typhoon of insanity, and I was ready for it to end. I would have walked right off a cliff if Gwen told me.

From the corner of my eye, I saw her raise the hand she held the remote in toward the speakers and press one of the buttons with her thumb. The opening riff to *Hole in the Sky* from Black Sabbath's *Sabotage* shot across the room from the speakers with tremendous clarity I only experienced for an instant before it became a muffled compressed drone in the back of my head, and the room turned a dull black and white.

I waited a few extra seconds before stepping forward. I didn't want to leave anything to chance and risk screwing the whole process up. I wanted to ensure the speakers had enough time to work their magic wholly and thoroughly before proceeding.

I looked at Gwen, still holding the remote toward my phone and the speakers. The smile was gone, replaced by a stern, hardened expression as she stared through the space my solid form had occupied moments ago. Ozzy's vocal kicked in on the song, and as he proclaimed, looking through a hole in the sky, I stepped through the wall.

Gwen was right about lights being the first thing I'd see, but the movement was too disorienting to tell if they were creating a tunnel. I felt a warmth flow through me and the sensation of floating in the ocean while waves pushed me in the direction I needed to go.

I didn't notice the music stopped. The cold started to set in a second later. The lights, the warmth, and the floating sensation were gone so fast that I wondered if I'd really been experiencing them. I continued moving slowly as instructed but found it much more difficult. Everything around me began to thicken to a density I found nearly impossible to push through until it was.

I was cold and disoriented. The spinning lights were gone, and I couldn't see anything. The music in my head had been replaced with the sound of rushing wind, and a cold stiffness worked through me. It was working. I was becoming completely whole again, and the curse the mysterious speakers brought with them was being pulled from every particle of my body.

My head began to ache from what felt like deep in the center of my brain. It was excruciatingly intense, but I guessed it was part of the process and gritted my teeth, waiting for it to pass. When it didn't, I tried to bring my hands up to massage the bridge of my nose, hoping to provide some relief, but I couldn't move my arms. I couldn't even feel them anymore.

I struggled to take the step I knew would bring me back through the wall and into my bedroom, but the effort was futile and confusing. Much like my arms, I couldn't feel my legs either. I opened my mouth to call out or thought I did, but it was as if all systems within me had gone offline. All I could feel was the pain and pressure continuing to build in my head, and I became startlingly aware something was going wrong with the procedure.

Suddenly, I could hear something again that sounded like the music. Despite the sensations I was experiencing, I must have been close to coming back through the wall. Maybe I was still moving, but it only felt like I wasn't because of whatever was going on to remove the curse. The music grew louder, and I felt relieved the whole experience was almost over. Whatever else there was to do when I got back had to be a piece of cake compared to this. Ozzy's vocals became loud enough for me to realize it wasn't Ozzy at all, and it wasn't a song I heard. It was laughter, Gwen's laughter.

"I'm sure you've realized by now that you will not be walking back through this wall." Gwen's voice boomed in my head with the same clarity the speakers gave to Black Sabbath. "There has been no one who has crossed Typhon, let alone stolen from me and lived. And not that it matters now, but there is no way to reverse a curse."

The name Typhon sounded familiar, and I wracked what little was left of my brain to remember where I knew it from, but the only thing I could associate it with was evil. I couldn't remember why, though. The pressure against my chest doubled, then tripled, making it nearly impossible to draw a breath, and my head felt heavy with the pain growing inside of it.

"I've been chasing this sand, my sand, for centuries. I can't believe they thought passing it off to someone like you under such ridiculous circumstances would keep me from finding it. All those before you have suffered. You are paying the ultimate price for stealing from the tomb I protect."

The voice in my head didn't sound like Gwen anymore, having taken on a lower register, growling through each word like a wild beast who'd learned to speak.

The word 'tomb' triggered a memory, and I saw an image of the charm on Gwen's necklace flash through my quickly petrifying mind. It was the same as the faint markings on the back of the speakers. There was a curse, only it wasn't what Gwen or Typhon led me to believe, but I understood now.

The pressure in my head rose to an unbearable intensity, and I wasn't cold anymore; I was freezing. As I continued to fuse with the wall, I felt my body being filled with sand, becoming gritty and heavy. The weight of the bricks crushed my bones and organs as the wall, and I became one.

Then, it all stopped, and I felt nothing. Somewhere far away, I heard Ozzy's voice demanding the hole in the sky take him to heaven. ☠

BOOKS & MAGAZINES

The Curses Collection
As Seen On T.V.
The Cycle
The Cadillac Man
Mage of the Hellmouth
Sinkhole
Death Pacts and Left-Hand Paths
Scummer
John Wayne Lied To You: A Mostly True
Account of the Adventures of a Modern Day Hero
Porn Star Retirement Plan
Charge Land
Aunt Poster
And Hell Followed: An Anthology
Breaking Bizarro
Broadswords and Blasters #3
Forbidden Futures #11

JOHN WAYNE COMUNALE

This author lives in the neon-drenched city of sin Las Vegas to prepare himself for the heat in Hell. He is the author of Death Pacts and Left-Hand Paths, Scummer, As Seen On T.V., Sinkhole, The Cycle, and more. He hosts the weekly storytelling podcast John Wayne Lied to You and fronts the punk rock disaster johnwayneisdead. He currently travels around the country, giving truly unique and most excellent performances of the written word.

ARTIST FOR THE FOLLOWING

Forbidden Futures Magazine
The Curses Collection
Teeth Where They Shouldn't Be
Death Goes to the Dogs
The Earthlings (author & artist)
Adventures with Immortality
Maxus
Scenes from a Village
Mystery Meat
The Wet Nurse and Other Tales
Professor Dario Bava
Weirdling
Morbid Curiosity
I Am A Barbarian
The Colour Out Of Space
The Call of Cthulhu

MIKE DUBISCH

This graphic novelist and illustrator has been creating and publishing comics and art since the 1980s. He has carved out a unique place creating horror, science-fiction, surrealism, and YA adventure works using all but lost traditional techniques. Born in California, USA, the artist has traveled and lived in five countries. He has been an instructor at the Academy Of Art University since 2012 and is married to children's book illustrator and sculptor Carolyn Watson Dubisch, with whom he has three daughters.

BOOKS & MAGAZINES

Forbidden Futures Magazine
The Curses Collection
Teeth Where They Shouldn't Be
Death Goes to the Dogs
The Earthlings
Adventures with Immortality
Maxus
Scenes from a Village
Mystery Meat
The Wet Nurse and Other Tales
The Inferno
The XXX Inferno
XYZZY

ODDNESS

This reclusive person (publisher, producer, editor) specializes in crafting captivating short story collections, novellas, and comics that transport readers to extraordinary realms is also the driving force behind Forbidden Futures magazine, where the fantastic and the unbelievable come to life.

Originating from unknown lands, ODDNESS dabbles in composing electronic music and playing video games.

www.ingramcontent.com/pod-product-compliance
Lightning Source LLC
Chambersburg PA
CBHW021549310726
48972CB00003B/750